# THE
# KEEPERS

## FILES 1.5
### A HOLDING KATE SERIES BOOK

## LaDonna Cole

PRODUCTIONS

Cover design, interior book design, all interior graphics, and eBook design by Blue Harvest Creative
*www.blueharvestcreative.com*

## The Keepers Files 1.5

Published by
HWV Productions

ISBN-13: 978-0-9912335-1-9
ISBN-10: 0991233514

Contact the author:

Facebook:
www.facebook.com/LaDonnaColeAuthor

Twitter:
www.twitter.com/Latidonna

Blog:
www.immortalportals.wordpress.com/author/ladonnacole

Websites:
www.heartworkvillage.com &
www.ladonnacolern.wix.com/ladonna-cole

Purchase other books by LaDonna Cole in print, eBook, or audio by scanning the QR code.

ALSO BY LaDONNA COLE

THE TORN
Book One
The Holding Kate Series

THE KEEPERS
Book Two
The Holding Kate Series
Coming Soon

DRUMMER BOY
A Family Christmas Story

*To the Musers,*
*the Keepers of my files*

# THE IMMORTAL SONG

*Hold me close, fly with me*
*Across immortal portals free.*
*Fall into the lover's sea.*
*With lips so full of worship.*

*I will hold you for all time.*
*Come and press your heart to mine.*
*With my promise on your breast*
*I live in your nearness.*

*Hold me fast, come let's go*
*Where fireflies bask in afterglow.*
*My kiss enfolds the tender soul*
*In bliss so full of worship.*

# REPORT

A FLASH OF lightning tossed shadow spikes through the dark office. Peals of thunder vibrated the weeping windows as the storm raged against the mansion. Mama Ty lifted weary eyes to the clock on the mantle.

1 AM.

She sighed, hit the print button and stood. Aching bones and strained muscles defined her last few years as administrator at Heartwork Village. She pressed her knuckles into the small of her back and kneaded at the coiled muscles. Stepping to the window, she peered through sheets of rain to Main Street. All the lights were out except for a small glow emanating through the stained glass windows of the chapel.

Chaplain Wright worked late most nights. This stormy one was no exception. *He's the man for the job*. A tough decision, she had the cowboy preacher or the ex-marine security chief, Charlie Goshen, to choose from as her temporary replacement. Both more than qualified for the job, they would do exactly as she asked, and more importantly, would ask few questions that she just couldn't answer.

*I'm getting ahead of myself,* she chided. She had planned for any contingency. This one was so far down the road that it lacked urgency to even consider at this point. Anything could happen between now and then. The printer spit out her letter and she picked it up to read it once more, checking for errors and typos.

722 Main Street
Heartwork Village, PA 17322

20960616

August Humphries
1 Palm Place Plaza Suite 3590
Anaheim, CA 90620

Dear Mr. August Humphries, Attorney at Law, and Trustees,

As requested, I have spent much time investigating the latest incidents here at Heartwork Village, in order to examine its risk and loss potential, possibility for legal and moral repercussions, as well as continued contribution to Chastain Corporation.

It is my firm opinion that the company is at risk of corporate espionage and our quantum sciences should have increased security measures implemented immediately. I have organized a task force to explore the possibility of subterfuge at the source level. The following report, dossiers, and memoirs will be accumulated from various employees, jumpers, and entities that are directly related to Heartwork Village and the quantum science that is practiced here. This report spans the three week training period the Keepers will receive. Subsequent reports will follow.

I will present the information to you in its raw form, leaving nothing out, so that you will understand the strength of their connections, the fastness of their bonds, and the depths of their love and respect for the process and for the team. After you have heard everything without censor, I will summarize my findings.

I believe this team to be specifically integral to the success of the mission. This packet will arrive after they are activated. Reports as to their success or failure will follow.

Warm regards,
Tylonica Abernathy, PhD,
Administrator, Heartwork Village

Mama Ty slipped the letter into the folder jacket with the resumes of the Keepers and dossiers of the Inner Circle. She would add the training reports over the next three weeks and then send the packet to corporate headquarters. The Keepers would be deep undercover by that time.

She carried the folder to the safe tucked behind a painting of three striking women and a young girl swallowed in a billow of red curls. A plaque attached to the bottom of the frame entitled it, *Four Souls*. Mama Ty stared at the painting for a long moment, then swung it out. She tapped the code into the keypad and a small section of the wall disappeared, revealing the safe. She tucked the file inside.

"Ale avèk Bondye," she murmured.

# THE KEEPERS FILES

THE KEEPERS TEAM is divided into two distinct groups. The first group consists of two teens and two twenty-year olds who traveled via quantum sphere into a jump that lasted 212 years. They gained invaluable life experience during that time. They are treated as adults and allowed to make decisions for themselves.

Name: Corey Chastain    DOB:   20790828   Jump Age: 229
Scriptorium Yrs: 1229

**Home:** Venice, Italy & Washington, D.C.
**Referral:** Self
**Jump Targets:** emanicipation
**Skills/Strengths:** multi talented, speaks four languages, musically inclined, black belts Karate and Tae Kwon Do, fencing
Jump Acquired S/S: medical, counseling, political, religious
**Position:** Team Leader
**Blood Type:** O pos
**Physical:** Superb
**Psychiatric Exam:** alert oriented, no trauma no self injurious thoughts, memory intact, judgment and insight excellent.

**Name:** Tara Johnson    **DOB:** 20800322    **Jump Age:** 228
**Scriptorium Yrs:** 231

**Home:** Aspen, Colorado
**Referral:** State of Colorado SVU
**Jump Targets:** lack of trust, socialization, bonding
**Skills/Strengths:** life-guard, ski expert, wilderness certification
**Jump Acquired S/S:** battle skills, leadership, weaponry
**Position:** Battle Chief, Weapons expert
**Blood Type:** AB negative
**Physical:** Superb
**Psychiatric Exam:** alert oriented, oppositional defiant, lacks social skills, judgment and insight good, tendency toward paranoid ideations, not pathological. Assaulted while hiking with friends, PTSD symptoms waning. Perpetrator caught and convicted due to her perseverence.

**Name:** Melanie Marcus  **DOB:** 20760517    **Jump Age:** 259
**Scriptorium Yrs:** 559

**Home:** Spring, Texas
**Referral:** Family, Heartwork Village Employee
**Jump Targets:** over protective
**Skills/Strengths:** Organizational Management, Leadership
**Jump Acquired S/S:** See employee file
**Position:** Jump Commander
**Blood Type:** O negative
**Physical:** Excellent
**Psychiatric Exam:** alert oriented, exceptional memory, euthymic, affect congruent, well balanced, judgment and insight good, thoughts linear, goal oriented, intelligent. Mel's family have all been involved as volunteers at HwV. She has been a valuable resource as a member of the staff.

**Name:** Donnie Dudgeon  **DOB:** 20750710     **Jump Age:** 259
**Scriptorium Yrs:** 559

**Home:** Spring, Texas
**Referral:** Family, Heartwork Village Employee
**Jump Targets:** sullen, moody, reactive attachment
**Skills/Strengths:** Tech skills, Extrapolates, Intelligence, Hand/Eye
**Jump Acquired S/S:** See employee file
**Position:** Jump Commander
**Blood Type:** A positive
**Physical:** Excellent
**Psychiatric Exam:** alert oriented, exceptional memory, euthymic, affect congruent, well balanced, judgment and insight good, thoughts linear, goal oriented. Donnie came to HwV as a jumper who spent most of his youth in various foster care situations. A friend of the Marcus family.

**Name:** Eunavae Montgomery  **DOB:** 208000126
**Jump Age:** 228  **Scriptorium Yrs:** 232

**Home:** Billings, Montana
**Referral:** Youth and Family Services
**Jump Targets:** self injurious behaviors, fire setting, victim of abuse
**Skills/Strengths:** forthright, loyal
**Jump Acquired S/S:** Bow, Medical, Music
**Position:** Alternate Keeper, Medic
**Blood Type:** AB negative
**Physical:** Excellent
**Psychiatric Exam:** PTSD, Intermittent Explosive Disorder, ADHD combined type

**Name: Katie Lynn Wilson  DOB: 20801212  Jump Age: 16
Scriptorium Yrs: 1016**

**Home:** Houston, Texas

**Referral:** Harris County Juvenile Services

**Jump Targets:** insecure, self esteem, divorce in family, indecisive

**Skills/Strengths:** intuitive, makes deep connections, empathy

**Jump Acquired S/S:** whip, confidence, forgiveness, loyalty

**Position:** Team Leader

**Blood Type:** A positive

**Physical:** Excellent

**Psychiatric Exam:** alert oriented, parent child relational, grief and loss, poor appetite, judgment fair and insight good. Kate came to HwV after defacing public property and drug charges were dropped in lieu of time spent at HwV. She is the product of a broken home.

**Name: Trip Carson  DOB: 20801022  Jump Age: 17
Scriptorium Yrs: 20**

**Home:** Austin, Texas

**Referral:** State of Texas Corrections Dept.

**Jump Targets:** anger, enmeshment, codependency, grief

**Skills/Strengths:** wrestling champ, letterman, sports

**Jump Acquired S/S:** battle skills, assassin, weaponry, strength

**Position:** Tactical Expert, hitter, guard

**Blood Type:** A positive

**Physical:** Superb

**Psychiatric Exam:** alert oriented, parent child bonding disorder, intermittent explosive disorder, oppositional defiant, judgment and insight good, post traumatic stress reaction.

Name: Dirk Johnson  DOB: 20731113  Jump Age: 49
Scriptorium Yrs: 57

**Home:** Princeton, New Jersey

**Referral:** DYFS, Employee of Heartwork Village

**Jump Targets:** gang violence, anger, addiction, loneliness

**Skills/Strengths:** leadership, analytical thinking, endurance

**Jump Acquired S/S:** see employee file

**Position:** Jump Commander

**Blood Type:** O positive

**Physical:** Superb

**Psychiatric Exam:** alert oriented, judgment and insight good, extrovert, euthymic, intelligent, memory intact, coping skills intact.

## FILE THREE

# THE SCIENCE

SHANNA STEPPED OUT onto the back porch dressed in khaki shorts, hiking boots, and a light blue t-shirt. Her hair sprayed from a pony tail, and she carried a small backpack with water and apples tucked inside. Rick sat on an Adirondack chair on the back porch waiting for her.

He stood and produced a ball cap out of his back pocket. "You are going to need this or your nose will burn." He set the cap on top of her head, took the backpack from her and swung it onto his shoulders.

Shanna pulled her ponytail through the back of the cap, slipped on her sunshades, and said, "Lead the way, Kemosabe."

Rick raised his eyebrows quickly twice and took Shanna's hand, leading her down the porch steps and out into the back woods.

The mammoth trees swayed in the gentle summer breeze and dappled sunlight played across the needle-strewn path. They walked slowly hand in hand for a long time, enjoying the forest sounds around them. The squirrels chattered in the vaulted limbs above them, and robins sang sweetly as the hikers passed beneath.

"You know, Shan, quantum theory is over a hundred years old, and we still don't understand much about it. I think I will restrict your education to how it applies to the event in the lake." Rick helped Shanna over a rocky ledge and then tucked her arm under his as they continued down the hill.

"Sounds good," Shanna agreed.

Rick took a deep breath. "There are five main ideas represented in quantum theory. One, energy is not continuous. It comes in small but discrete units."

Shanna nodded.

"Two, there are particles and there are waves." He checked to see if she followed. "Three, these particles move randomly, by their nature. Four, it is physically impossible to know both the position and the momentum of a particle at the same time. In fact, the more you know about one, the less you can know about the other."

"Uh hmm." Shanna furrowed her brow.

"Five, the atomic world is nothing like the world we live in."

"Well, at least I can grasp number five." Shanna smiled.

Rick chuckled. "Okay, so if you observe these particles and waves, they blink into existence, otherwise they continue on about their random wanderings."

"The filthy strumpets," Shanna piped.

"Yes, well." Rick gave her a playful frown. "Anyway, if you observe one of these subatomic particles, it becomes manifest."

"What do you mean if you observe it, then it becomes?"

"Well, if you perform an experiment, say, and observe a random movement of the subatomic particle or wave, then it becomes what you observed. Otherwise it is happy to continue in its indefinable state."

"Whoa, that is really weird!"

"You think?" Rick cocked his head wondering if he explained it poorly. "All of these particles are linked somehow. They seem to know where the other ones are. There is an unknown element that ties together all subatomic particles."

"So this is scientific theory, not just science fiction?" Shanna stopped in her tracks.

"Yes, Shan, the greatest minds that existed studied quantum physics: Albert Einstein, Niels Bohr, Max Planck. This isn't just a freaky alien TV show."

"So you're saying that my father had an experience at the lake and sought to explain it through science." Shanna started to feel a release in her chest.

They came to a large boulder situated under a sprawling oak overlooking a secluded crescent-shaped meadow. Rick hopped up on the boulder and then lifted Shanna to join him. He shrugged off the backpack and fished out two water bottles. Shanna took off her sunglasses and tucked one handle down the front of her t-shirt and pulled off her cap. They each took a swig from the water bottles and twisted the lids back on. Shanna pulled her knees up under her chin and rested her head on them, arms wrapped tightly around her shins.

She sat in that position watching the wildflowers in the meadow sway with the breeze and cloud shadows shift across the field. Her mind found solace in the thought that her father had not been crazy after all. Which meant this handsome and affectionate man sitting next to her was probably not crazy either. She sighed, relieved at both prospects.

"So your theory is what, that somehow through these subatomic particles you can hear a woman singing from another county or state?"

"Or dimension."

"Dimension?" Shanna backpedaled toward crazy again.

"Remember, the atomic world is nothing like our world. It is possible that another dimension of reality exists side by side with our own."

"So a woman in another dimension can be heard singing in our pond because of quantum physics?"

"In theory, because remember, all particles and waves are interconnected." Rick spoke softly with several pauses. She was glad. It allowed the words to find a resting place in her mind and imagination before he rushed to another wild theory.

Shanna turned her head and rested her cheek on her knee and studied Rick. His face was deeply tanned, and he had tiny creases starting in the corners of his eyes. He returned her gaze with interest and intensity.

"The woman in the lake is there, because Dad observed her." Shanna's lower lip quivered and she leaned into Rick. "Confusing."

He wrapped his arm around her and she rested her head in the crook of his arm. He pulled her tightly against himself and kissed her hair. They comforted each other with soft words and caresses and let the shared loss of her dad become a lighter burden in the sharing.

They reclined on the sofa for a long time very aware of the savory tension swirling in the air around them. Rick wrapped his arm around Shanna's waist and pulled her close, covering her arm with his and entwining his fingers through hers, his hand protectively enclosing her hand. Shanna stared at their hands for awhile, watching the pulse in his veins slow gradually.

"Tell me more about quantum theory," Shanna hummed, craning her neck around toward him.

"Okay," he spoke softly and leaned down to kiss her ear. "Well, did you know that every subatomic particle is made of superstrings? They are tiny donut-shaped dots of energy that spin at a frequency or vibrate on a pitch." His breath warmed her ear.

"Like a song?" She lifted her head into his whispered caresses.

"Yeah, of course they aren't real in this dimension until someone observes them. Then the quantum wave or particle collapses by that observation, we call it popping a qwiff."

"Popping a qwiff," Shanna reiterated, almost a hum.

"Yeah, so when you pop a qwiff, you observe the particle singing and it becomes something in our reality."

"So basically hearing the particle song causes something to cross into our dimension?"

"That is the theory, well in its most basic, simplistic, and-completely-elementary-to-the-point-of-really-showing-a-complete-lack-of-understanding form."

"Well, as long as I am truly getting it, right?" Shanna joked.

"Right." Rick grinned and pulled her tighter to him.

"This reminds me of something I heard in Mass once."

"Seriously, your priest was versed in quantum theory?" Rick chuckled.

"No, I doubt it. But he said one time that the Bible said to call those things that are not, as though they were, and then he said something about 'God has chosen things which are invisible to zero out those things which are visible.'"

"Sounds like quantum theory to me," Rick agreed.

"Hmmm." Shanna sat there deep in thought, trying to make sense of everything. Quantum this and qwiff that jumbled around in her brain. She felt she had a very basic understanding of what Rick knew and not quite sure she bought into the whole quantum theory as a science thing. But truth rang through the words that she could not explain.

*©Excerpt from Threshold, Tsian the Wise, Sisterhood of the Sword Saga, by LaDonna Cole*

# ORIGINS

HEARTWORK VILLAGE IS a Residential Recovery facility for teens who have had difficulty with transition or who have experienced great loss. The village has utilized quantum technology through stabilized jump spheres that was developed over the last 100 years. The spheres carry the facility residents in teams through obstacles that bring them to a place of recovery through emotive educational experiences.

The scientist credited for the discovery of the quantum veil is Richard J. Wilson, PhD, who pioneered the science of sphere mechanics in quantum streaming. He was a tenured professor at Georgetown University and lived in First Cabin with his wife Shanna Wisenberg Wilson, the first known person to cross into another dimension through the quantum veil.

## TSIAN'S CROSSING

Shanna woke late in the night. She was hot and sweaty pressed against Rick. The fire had died down but the room still blazed. Carefully slipping out from under Rick's arm, not wanting to wake him, Shanna crept to the front door and opened it to let in some of the breeze.

The cool night air hit her face and buffeted her hair away from her sticky neck. She stretched and enjoyed the refreshing breeze. Stepping out onto the porch, she yawned, drawing the cooling draft deeply into her lungs. She turned to go back inside when she heard it.

Shanna stilled and listened. The wind rushed through the trees and the crickets played their accompaniment. She had just about convinced herself that she had heard nothing when the wind carried the lyrical refrain to her again.

It was music. She glanced in all directions wondering if a radio or something played but could not locate the source of the sound. She listened more intently to the strangest music she had ever heard. Sounds in frequencies that should not be possible to hear with the human ear trilled through the grass and onto the porch where she listened. Intermingled in the music harmonized a crashing surf, a choir of children's voices, a deep guttural rending, a tinkling high-pitched crystal, the fracturing of an iced-over lake, and the music! Oh! A woman's voice resounded in ethereal tones. So hauntingly compelling, it rose in waves of ecstasy and descended to near whispered refrain. The song defined beauty and purity, life and light.

*Light*? Shanna tilted her head as the pond drew her focus. A blue glow in the center of the lake pulsed in cadence with the song. Bare feet whispered in the dewy grass as she made her way to the pier and strained to see the phenomenon.

Curious and wanting to investigate, she stepped into the fishing boat, released the docking rope, and rowed to the center of the lake where the pulsing luminescence throbbed rhythmically with the enchanting voice of the lady.

She rowed directly over the blue light and back paddled to bring the boat to a stop. Setting down the oar, she leaned over to gaze into the cerulean incandescence. The glow beamed out of the lake onto her face, revealing a mirrored image in the water, dancing with the ripples as the music vibrated the surface of the pool.

What should have been her own reflection startled her. She gasped and threw her hand up to touch her face.

The image in the water mimicked her motions and expression, but the face reflecting back to her was that of a child of about 8 years. Shanna leaned closer to better see this strange spectacle. She reached out her hand toward the surface and saw that the child reached toward her in echo. The music pulsed and danced around her and called to her with a very primal intensity. Feeling timeless, as young as a babe and as ancient as time itself, Shanna felt drawn inexplicably to the girl in the night lake.

Stars danced in the ripples around the mystical and magical child of light. The otherworldly music drew at her spirit, compelling her to be noble, pure, and whole. Tears ran down Shanna's cheeks as the music washed over her soul in waves of truth, peace, and love. She had never felt this before. She had never known such a pure and true love. She could not get enough of it. It broke over her, filling her spirit to the point she thought she would not be able to take anymore or she would burst into pure energy, and yet the song continued and the infilling continued, growing ever deeper. It filled her so completely that there was no corner or crevice of her heart that had not been scoured, illuminated, and filled with holy presence.

She longed to touch the child. She seemed so real, yet so surreal. They stretched their hands to one another. When Shanna's palm broke the surface of the numinous pool, a mighty force latched onto her and wrenched her from the boat. She pierced the plane of the lake, drawn deeper and deeper into the cerulean light song.

She knew she should struggle, fight for life, but the deep blue was too compelling and it drew her down and deeper into its pulsating warmth. The thought crossed her mind that she was probably dying, but the blanket of peace wrapping her prevented all alarm. She willingly and eagerly drew the liquid into her lungs, drinking the tranquility in insatiable gratitude.

*Soon I will be with father*, she reasoned, not afraid of that prospect. The blue song wrapped her tightly in a cocoon of wholeness, love, and healing peace. Shanna knew joy and crossed over.

Rick woke at the sound of the crickets and shivered. He sat up expecting to see Shanna nearby. She was not. The door stood wide open. He pushed himself off of the couch and walked out onto the porch. Something on the lake caught his eye. The moon's blue glow seemed radiant and illuminated someone in the boat. He squinted his eyes and focused through the mist that crept along the shoreline. A flash of strawberry blond curls whipped in the breeze and he realized Shanna was in the boat on the lake. He walked down the path to the pier and strained to see what she was doing. Just as he got to the end of the pier, she leaned over the edge of the boat and fell into the water.

He laughed. "Shan, what are you doing out here?" *Crazy girl, serves you right, getting out in the middle of the night.* He expected her to break to the surface sputtering and spewing water any second. She did not resurface.

"Shan?" He began to get worried. The blue light died down and faded and he realized that it was not just the reflection of the moon on the water. It must have been the event, the quantum flux. "Shanna!" Rick dove in the water and swam wildly toward the boat. "Oh God! Shanna!" he shouted.

He reached the boat and began diving and frantically searching for her. Again and again he dove, scrambled around in the inky blackness to find her and returned to the surface empty handed. His muscles ached with the repeated exertion and deprivation of oxygen. He stayed under longer each time, hating to leave the bottom without her safely in his arms. His lungs burned and demanded that he come up for air. He broke the surface and gulped oxygen. Hopelessness descended on him and ravaged the tender places of his heart that had just begun to love. "Shanna!" he sobbed and gasped for breath that would not bring relief to the suffocating pressure on his chest. His heart shattered. "Shanna!" He drew a deep breath and dove once again.

©*Excerpt from Threshold, Tsian the Wise, Sisterhood of the Sword Saga, by LaDonna Cole*

(A more detailed account of her years in the alternate location can be found in The Chronicles of Ampeliagia.)
Another early crossing through the quantum veil occurred years later.

## VALEN'S JOURNEY

"Mimi!" Valen ran through the screen door of the boat house screeching. "Mimi, Papaw!"

"Whoa there, youngster." Rick snagged his granddaughter's arm. "What's all this excitement?"

"Papaw! I saw the deer family! I saw the mommy deer and the two little fawns!" Valen bounced into her grandfather's arms.

"You did? In the meadow?"

"Yes, Papaw! We have to tell Mimi! She loves the baby deer!"

Rick laughed and touched the freckled cheek of his five year old grandchild, visiting for the summer. She favored his wife, Shanna. Red spiraled curls and mischievous green eyes shined.

"Mimi!" The screen door slammed behind Shanna.

Rick gazed at his bride, she still stole his breath. Hair piled in a messy knot of curls and glasses perched on the end of her nose, she sauntered to the worktable where dusty artifacts littered every inch of space and old books piled high in towers. A sarcophagus leaned against the wall and straw-filled crates spilled open.

Shanna broke into his favorite smile when Valen's excitement reached her. "Hello, my two favorite people!" Shanna enveloped Valen and kissed her nose. "What's all the commotion?"

"I saw them, Mimi! You said if I sat very still and quiet, they would come! They did, Mimi! They did!"

Shanna clapped her hands together with sheer glee. "Oh Valen, I'm so glad you got to see them!" She escorted Valen to the worn leather sofa.

Rick settled beside them and listened to Valen chatter. He and Shan stole smoldering glances over her head. Resting his arm along the back of the couch, he fingered Shan's curls while she listened to Valen's account of the fawn's antics.

Before long Valen finished her story and wandered away to another adventure.

Rick stroked Shanna's cheek, she flushed under his touch like a schoolgirl. It reminded him of the moment he fell in love with her.

"I want to show you something." Taking his hand, she led him to the table. "Look at this piece."

"It's beautiful." He fingered the workmanship of the pewter vase.

"It isn't Terran."

Rick locked his eyes on Shanna. "You mean..."

"It's Ampeliagian, Rick."

He furrowed his brow. "Are you sure?"

"Test it with your quantum EMF."

"I will." He turned the vase over in his hands, inspecting it from every angle. "I didn't think things could cross to this side of the veil."

Rick dragged Shan and the vase to his side of the boat house. Pushing aside the large vinyl strips separating the lab from her artifacts, they stepped into his world of shiny surfaces and beakers. Computers lined one wall and a table of electronic and magnetic measuring instruments mirrored it.

He analyzed the vase and shared a grin with Shanna when the needle spiked into the quantum range.

"It's the same material as your ring," he confirmed. "It's truly from Ampeliagia." Shanna nodded and her gray curls bounced against her cheek.

They were so engrossed in their work that they didn't notice the sunset or passing of time.

"Where is Valen?" Shanna stretched.

Rick looked up absentmindedly from his computer. "Huh? I don't know. It isn't like her to be away so long."

"Rick!" Shanna's face sketched worried lines and her voice weakened with dread.

"Don't worry, honey, she is probably watching TV. Let's go see."

Walking along the dock, Shanna paused, then pointed. "Rick!"

The canoe bobbed abandoned midway in the glassy pond. "Don't panic, Shan. Go check the house."

Shanna sprinted, calling "Valen! Valen!"

Rick thrashed to the center of the pond. Tilting the canoe toward him, he peered inside. Valen's daisy flip flop lay abandoned in the bottom.

The screen door slammed. Shanna sped to the pier's foot, peeling off her clothes. "She isn't answering!" White skin pierced black water. Diving and searching, praying and hoping, they desperately groped for their precious granddaughter in the recessed depths.

Memories assailed Rick. Thirty years ago this had happened, except Shan was the one missing. She had crossed over into another world, Ampeliagia, and lived several years as the foster daughter of a great king, the companion to three exceptional women, and servant to a god she curiously called Juan.

Once again, he sought a redheaded girl who had stolen his heart, but this one was his own flesh and blood. Plunging deeper each time, he penetrated the mysterious lake. The moon and stars danced across the ripples, beauty mocking the frenetic search.

What if he failed this time?

No, he would not lose Valen.

After thirty minutes his muscles screamed in agony and he knew Shan was exhausted. He sent her to the pier.

"Rick, it's been too long. She couldn't—" Shanna's voice broke with the dread of her own words.

Rick dove again refusing to give up. His lungs seared in his chest and with a mouthful of water he surrendered to the surface.

"Rick!"

Shan's voice wasn't coming from the dock or the canoe as he expected.

"Rick!"

Scouring the edges of the shadowy pond, he caught a snatch of white between the reeds.

"Rick, help me." Shanna, in the thick of the reeds curved over something. "Rick, I found her!"

"Dear God." He splashed toward Shanna's voice. She bent over the frail form and puffed into her mouth.

Rick slogged into the shallows and collapsed beside the lifeless body of his granddaughter. "Shanna, is she?"

"She has a pulse. She's not breathing." Shanna blew another breath.

The chest of Rick's tiny grandbaby rose and fell as Shanna forced air into her lungs. Willing his grand-daughter to live, he cried into his fists.

Breathe.

He waited an eternity.

Water lapped along the shore.

Shanna forced air.

A bat fluttered across the sky.

Shanna forced breath.

A toad plunked into the water.

Shanna forced life.

Valen's hand fluttered and she coughed.

"Thank you, Juan," Shanna whispered and cradled Valen upright.

Valen retched volumes of water.

"For my babies," Valen's voice croaked. "For my twin boys."

Her eyes focused on the faces hovering above her and registered alarm. "Where am I?" she rasped out.

"Valen, honey, you're here with Mimi and Papaw. You're okay, we saved you." Shanna cooed and smoothed Valen's hair.

Rick's blood ran cold in his veins. The expression on his granddaughter's face, he had seen before on his wife.

"Bor!" Valen's little voice moaned in grief too deep for her years.

Rick buried his face in his hands.

"Bailen, Achbor!" Her mourning cries broke the stillness of the night.

Shanna's startled gasp drew Rick's gaze.

"Did you say Achbor?" she whispered.

"My son! Do you know where he is?" Valen seized Shanna's arms and implored. "Regolian will kill him. We must hide them both."

Shanna made a popping sound in the back of her throat and her eyes slid out of focus.

"She crossed." Shanna trembled in shock. "She crossed over. She was Achbor's mother."

Rick scooped his granddaughter into his arms and led his wife into the house.

"I can't believe it. Achbor told me once I reminded him of his mother, Valen. I'd completely forgotten about it." Shanna gaped at her granddaughter. "She lived a lifetime in Ampeliagia, she'll never be the same. She's not a child anymore."

"If anyone can help her through this it is you. Think of the bond you'll share. You both loved a great king, her son, your foster father."

Shanna fingered the burgundy ringlets splayed across Valen's face and longing flashed across hers. She was homesick for Ampeliagia. Rick determined in that moment to find a way to open the door between the two worlds.

*©Excerpt from A Story and a Cup of Tea, by LaDonna Cole*

It was these two very separate, yet similar, quantum anomalies that drove Dr. Richard Wilson to create a stable transport across quantum worlds. He succeeded and Emotive Educational Quantum Jumps birthed from his work.

FILE FIVE
# THE INNER CIRCLE

HEARTWORK VILLAGE QUANTUM jumps are strictly monitored by a team of professional scientists, psychiatric and mental health providers, spiritual leaders, and fitness and wellness experts. These professionals are known as the Inner Circle and are maintained in a top secret facility and they will serve one year in a rotation. Each member of the Inner Circle is screened, processed, and approved by a team of psychiatrists and testing specialists. They are interconnected by a matrix that runs an algorithm of the Inner Circle's thought processes and chooses sphere destinations in various time/spatial/dimension locations. Safety protocols are in place which circumnavigate the jumpers into other worlds and keep them from going into the past of our dimension to prevent time paradoxes. Also safety protocols prevent dangerous or life threatening situations so that optimal recovery is possible.

However, something has gone horribly wrong with the Inner Circle. The safety protocols are no longer working. Jumpers are sent into perilous, life threatening conditions and put through grueling tasks that have resulted in loss of life and have had a deep psychological impact on the teens who have survived.

Tylonica Abernathy formed a task force to investigate the possibility that one of the Inner Circle is sabotaging the safety protocols and purposely sending jumpers into peril.

It is with great concern and trepidation that we enter into this investigation to ferret out the culprit who is attempting to sabotage the good work of Heartwork Village. At the beginning of this investigation the following twelve professionals serve as the Inner Circle. The professionals are listed in the month order of their rotation. Each month, a member of the circle is released and another takes his/her place to serve for one year. These are the outstanding scientists in the current Inner Circle.

The Inner Circle as of 6-23-2096

## January

### Dossier of Dr. Lahiri Mutsuddi
#### Dhaka, Bangledesh

Bioengineer, for Merztech Corp for 11 years in The People's Republic of Bangladesh, pioneered groundbreaking work in duplicate genetic streaming.

Published in *Science Weekly*, regular contributor to *Genetech Quarterly*

**Religion:** Buddhist
**Marital Status:** Married

### Other Information

Worked closely with Heartwork Village Engineers to perfect the quantum stasis fields for replication interfaces for the last 7 years

## February

### Dossier of Dr. Lesa Prackovnik
#### Czech Republic

Brilliant holo engineer who completed groundbreaking work in the field of Quantum stasis and molecular manipulation through nanorobotics.

Celebrated and published in *Robotics Today, NanoTech Weekly, Science Weekly*.

Tenured at Harvard School of Science and Technology

**Religion:** No Affiliation
**Marital Status:** Divorced, no children

### Other Information

Dr. Prackovnik spent five years in a holodome of her creation with 8 volunteers for the research. So intricate was her holoprogramming and duplication, they did not know they were in a dome and continued to believe they were in the real world carrying on their lives.

## March

### Dossier of Dr. Akio Fujitani
Kyoto, Japan

Specializes in Extraterrestrial tectonics and Atmoshperic Physics. Geophysicist and Meteorologist.

Published in *Weather Outlook, Who's Who on What Planet,* and authored *Aliens Rock, a Geology Survey of Venus.*

**Religion:** Scientology
**Marital Status:** Married, four children

### Other Information

Traveled extensively through sphere technology to other planets to collect specimen geodes. He owns the Rock House, a museum with the largest collection of alien geodes.

## April

### Dossier of Dr. June Pascavis, MD
Montreal, Canada

Widely published thesis on Biomolecular Physics and effects of quantum shifts on the cellular construct of life forms.

Published in *Health Today, I-Med Medical Blog* columnist, Most eligible scientist, *People Magazine's* top 100 beautiful people.

**Religion:** Jewish
**Marital Status:** Single

### Other Information

Played a vital role in early research of the effects of sphere science on the human body, only has one mutation as a result of her research.

## May

### Dossier of Keelan Keating, PhD
Kilkenny, Ireland

Specializing in Abnormal Psychiatry and Adolescent Psychology. Worked as Medical Director for Columbus International Behavioral Health for 10 years.

Published in *Psychology Today*, Dr. Phil's top 10 referrals.

**Religion:** Methodist
**Marital Status:** Divorced

### Other Information
Key participant in developing Heartwork Village Curriculum.

## June

### Dossier of Dr. Spivey Carrington, DMV, PhD
Sydney, Australia

Veterinarian, Zoologist, Mammalogist, and Outback Survival Specialist. Innovative work in species identification. Touted as the first scientist to prove the existence of a colony of Sasquatch in the Pack Forest of Washington State, USA.

**Religion:** Pitjatjatjara Mysticism
**Marital Status:** Single

### Other Information
Collaborated with geneticists to design the infamous Blue Monkey species who can be found on the Island of Patmos, in the jungles of Fazebukistan, and various other locations.

## July

### Dossier of Rev. Liz Robertson, MDiv, DMin
#### Los Angeles, California

Highly acclaimed faith healer, author, and prophetess. The current spiritual link in the Inner Circle.

Writer of *The Azuza Movement*, and *From Faith to Freedom*, and listed as Best Selling author on NY Times list for three months for her Autobiography, *Lizzie's Last Breath*.

**Religion:** Interdenominational
**Marital Status:** Married, three children

### Other Information

Hosts the annual Jesus for President Rallies in Pittsburg, PA.

## August

### Dossier of Dr. Gregorvitch Mattovdzky, PhD,
#### Quantum Mechanics
#### Garwolin, Poland

Developed technology for stabilizing the Quantum Spheres using constant molecular motion to enhance the wall integrity of the transport.

**Religion:** Jewish
**Marital Status:** Single

### Other Information

Added inert chemical process to increase shield integrity of radiation barriers

## September

### Dossier of Xiomar Kunkel, MD, PhD
Berlin, Germany

Computer Programmer and Analyst holds Doctorate in Computer Mechanics and Technology from MIT and Bioengineering Doctorate from Harvard School of Medicine.

**Religion:** Baptist
**Marital Status:** Married, one child

### Other Information

Worked closely with Heartwork Village Information Systems to create interface between Inner Circle and Quantum Matrix.

## October

### Dossier of Dr. Karfelt Pazicni, PhD
Dallas, Texas from the Rom Gypsy clan

Touted with the discovery of intellectual streaming through Quantum Mechanics. Perfected the interactive matrix linking individual imagination to a hive imagination to produce creative molecular cohesion.

**Religion:** Christian Pentecostal
**Marital Status:** Married, six children

### Other Information

Worked with Heartwork Village medics in initial phases of psychic connection theory.

## November

### Dossier of Putney Harnist, PhD
#### Geneva, Switzerland

Research Psychologist specializing in the psychological effect of Quantum Shifting on brain chemistry.

Published in *Psychology Today, Mind Over Matter Magazine, Freudian Follies.*

**Religion:** Catholic
**Marital Status:** Married, no children

### Other Information

Published research on the effects of Quantum science in addition to regular curriculum of therapy and grief recovery. His findings led to funding for Heartwork Village technologies.

## December

### Dossier of Dr. Kilgore Buzard, MD
#### Paris, France

Highly acclaimed nutrition, exercise, and health trainer. Holds Certification in Holistic Medicine, Personal Trainer, Dietician.

Wrote *Healthy Lifestyle Made Simple,* and *Foods that Fool,* and *Fountain of Youth.*

**Religion:** Charismatic Catholic
**Marital Status:** Divorced, no children

### Other Information

Worked with Heartwork Village to develop menu choices for the village and sustainable nutrition options in quantum jumps.

Quantum Perspective Source:

A QPS is a moment or set of actions in the Quantum Stream that allows a decision to be recorded. These junctions are intersections that are captured by specific quantum measurement and can be played back for review. Many quantum scientists theorize that at each decision point, any decision that could be made, is made and a new dimension forms. While searching for proof of these alternate realities, scientists discovered a quantum bank of these decisions. They labeled them Quantum Perspective Sources as they are specific to the decision maker and center around those decisions.

# QPS:
# EYE ON THE PRIZE

"THERE JUST ISN'T enough here, Corey." Kate pushed back from the computer terminal and rubbed her eyes.

We had been at it for 18 hours straight and we still felt we only had a cursory understanding of the psyche of the Inner Circle.

I rolled my chair over to her and gently started massaging her back and neck muscles. I planted a kiss on her forehead as she leaned her head back toward me.

"Mmmm," she sighed and stretched her neck.

I thought of the day I first saw her. The day my life changed forever.

The limo dropped me off at the Village and drove away. I watched the taillights until Giles, my chauffeur, disappeared around the corner.

An enormous black man greeted me. "Heya, I'm Dirk, are you Corey Chastain?" He checked a clipboard.

"Yeah, that's me." I bumped his fist.

"You're the first one here, so I dub thee Number One, keeper of the luggage." He knighted my shoulders with his pencil.

I was glad that Dad's lawyer talked me into coming here as a jumper. I would be able to see exactly how things worked and not have to deal with the prestige issues that came with my family ties.

As the cars arrived, I helped Dirk with the luggage and introductions. One guy about my age showed up in handcuffs with his parole officer.

Dirk and I walked out to meet them on the blacktop. "Those won't be necessary," Dirk said pointing to the handcuffs.

The parole officer shrugged. "Suit yourself." He keyed the cuffs then handed Dirk some paperwork. I jerked my head indicating the boy should follow me.

"I'm Corey." I offered my hand.

"Trip Carson." He shook my hand and jerked his long bangs out of his face.

I introduced him to some of the other guys and they stood and ogled a tall blond who had just arrived. My attention was caught by another recent arrival. She wrapped her slender arms around her mother and I saw her face break into deep sorrow, but when she pulled back she rearranged her features into a brave smile for her mother.

I watched the beautiful girl as Kim, a breezy redhead in a STAFF shirt, approached them. The new arrival's long dark hair tickled her back and draped over her slight frame as it wafted in the breeze. Her every movement was a song, a work of art.

Kim waved Dirk over and he called for me to help him. I was more than glad to get a closer look. I jogged over and Kim introduced us. My face wouldn't stop grinning as I looked into her beautiful brown eyes and saw a kindred heart.

Dirk was saying something, I saw them bump hands and immediately felt a pang of longing to touch that creamy pale skin.

"Hey," I gawked with a stupid grin on my face.

Her pupils dilated and she lifted the corner of her mouth. I fastened my gaze on her full and beautiful lips, then back to her emotive eyes. I didn't think I had ever seen a face so fragile, so perfect, so open and vulnerable.

I never believed in love at first sight. Heck, I had never really believed in love, but in that moment all of my beliefs crumbled like wedding cake around my feet. I lifted her luggage and couldn't get past the thought that her hands had touched these very bags.

I was smitten. In that one fraction of time, my world turned on its side and I would never be the same. Kate Wilson had entered it.

I watched her closely all through orientation, I knew she was right behind me. I even thought I saw her look at me at one point. Trip had somehow latched onto her too. He kept touching her and it bothered me.

I managed to stand close to her when we met our jump commanders, Mel and Donnie. She even looked at me once and we shared a shy little smile. *Glorious day, Kate smiled at me! Ugh, I am such a creeper!*

After we were fitted for our jump suits, I noticed her frail form as she danced out into the commons area. Her every move was graceful and feminine. I had the urge to touch her hair as she walked past me to speak to Trip.

I finagled my way to sit across from her at dinner, thinking we might have a chance to talk, but she and Trip were engaged in a strange flirtatious conversation, so I turned to the people around me and spoke with them.

At the fireside show-and-tell I watched her as she lavished her delicate attention on her new friend with the pink hair. My heart strained toward her, wanting to be closer so I could hear her voice. Trip leaned against her shoulder possessively.

I was surprised at Trip's reaction to her. He was busy ogling the tall blond when Kate arrived and didn't even seem to notice her until just before we left the parking lot.

When we were finally chosen as partners for the Scriptorium, my heart danced inside of me. I would finally have some time alone with this beautiful and delicate creature.

Ha! *Time alone?* We spent a thousand years with one another. It was the beginning of the union of our souls. I was already in love with her, but in the Scriptorium I fell in love with who she was, not just what she looked like. She opened up to me, cried over her family and little brother. I stroked her cheek and wiped her tears, kissed away her sorrow. We held each other for an eternity. I never tired of the feel of her skin or the sound of her voice. I memorized every part of her face and fleck in her eyes. She had a tiny little scar on her chin and I kissed it and asked her about it. She told me a funny story about a chicken attacking her. Her laughter was a sparkling of bubbles and sound. I found myself telling jokes just to hear her laugh. I told her about SpongeBob in a sushi bar and she giggled so hard she lost her breath.

She became my world, my life. My heart melded into hers and we became one holding each other, singing, sharing, and rolling in pink clouds. Kate was a gift, a treasure, everything I ever wanted or needed.

After a thousand years, we returned to the cruel reality of Trip. Kate pulled away from me as though our thousand years of love were merely a dream.

I worked the tense muscles out of Kate's neck until she pushed away from the computer terminal, stood up, and kissed me.

"Thank you, Corey," she whispered and her eyes lit up the way they did only for me.

"Let's take a break. We can come back to it after a bite to eat and a nap." I hugged her off the floor, whirled her around, and we walked hand in hand to our makeshift kitchen.

We had been given the use of 3 rooms in the underground facility while we trained. The girls stayed in one room and the boys in another, much to the dismay of Mel and Donnie who had lived as husband and wife for 210 years. We turned the room between us into a common gathering room and make-shift kitchen.

We entered the room and found Dirk and Trip in discussion about battle tactics. "Hey," I greeted them.

Kate went to the fridge and stuck her head in. I watched Trip cut his eyes over to Kate as she rummaged through the veggie drawer.

"It's getting pretty scant in here," Kate called and held up a wilted head of lettuce and a squishy looking cucumber.

"Dirk ordered dinner. Mama Ty is sending us takeout from Taky Tako," Trip answered.

"Moo goo gai pan?" Kate's eyebrows shot to the ceiling. It was her favorite.

"Of course," Trip laughed.

Kate grabbed a juice bottle and shook it at me. I nodded and she tossed it to me, grabbed another, and we sat down across from Dirk and Trip.

"How is the research coming?" Dirk asked.

Kate wrinkled her nose. Trip couldn't take his eyes off of her. I leaned over and gathered her under my arm. "Well , I can tell you what each of their college GPAs were, what they scored on their ACTs and MATs, I can even tell you their blood types, but we need some personal information and it just isn't in the database."

Kate snuggled into my shoulder and I pulled her tighter to me. Trip frowned and looked away. It was probably a good reminder for him that Kate was *my* girlfriend. I had the feeling I had given him too much liberty with her.

Don't get me wrong. Kate was free to choose her own way, and I know she loved me eternally. I was just not sure Trip really understood our bond. I think he imagined his bond was equally strong with her.

We had given Kate freedom to come and go between us as her heart led her. We knew that would be essential to her survival and to getting us all safely out of the jumps as we engaged in quantum espionage to find the infiltrator in the Inner Circle. I didn't want her feeling guilty for acting on emotions that were necessary.

I think there was a bit of arrogance in my decision, too. I knew Kate loved me and I underestimated how much Trip loved her and how that would affect her. I thought he and Tara had something pretty special, but so far Trip's deference to Kate indicated that his feelings for Tara were less defined.

"...her mom is livid, of course!" Mel and Tara came around the corner with a breezy redhead named Kim Stevens carrying sacks of Chinese takeout. "But she isn't even allowed to see her for another 3 weeks."

"Yay!" Kate perked up. "Food!"

We spread the food out across the table and began to chopstick our way through the wide selection.

Kim had moved into our cabin at Heartwork Village to take Mel and Donnie's place. She filled us in on our teammates and their progress toward acclimating to life as teenagers again.

"Catilyn and Navarro are still grieving their children," she spoke softly. "They refuse to be separated, and frankly I didn't have the heart to insist. I set them up in my room, and I took Caitlyn's bunk with Eunavae in the girl's dorm."

"I know how they feel," Donnie grumbled. Mel leaned into his shoulder.

"None of them took the news well that they had been erased from the memories of their descendants."

My heart was heavy for my family of teammates. None of us would ever be the same. The 200 year jump changed us entirely. Only Kate and Trip escaped that fate. They hadn't been near us when we jumped, so they stayed at the village. I couldn't leave her behind, though. She was present as though she lived on my skin. I would close my eyes at night and picture her face, her gold flecked eyes, her hair as it spilled around her shoulders, and I would remember the scent of her. Every night for 2 centuries, I imagined my Kate. I began to tell the story hoping to purge myself of the overwhelming sensation that she was still with me. After decades, my stories became legend, a whole religion developed around the tale of Kate of a Thousand Years and the deity who held us.

We finally came home, but were adults suddenly constrained by teenage rules. Except for Trip and Kate who had not been on the jump with us, they actually were still teenagers. I couldn't really count the thousand year Scriptorium as life experience. That was just pure bliss, with Kate and clouds. Trip and Kate were closer in real time age. I wondered if that was part of their continued attraction. Maybe I had just become too mature for Kate. I hoped that wasn't the case.

The conversation drifted to Jewel City, our settlement in the 212 year jump, as it usually did. It was hard to stay in the present when it was such a small percentage of our total life experience.

"His hands were as big as dinner plates!" Mel exclaimed.

"Oh! They were not!" Tara moaned.

"Bran was enormous, you have to admit it, Tara!" I threw a fortune cookie at her.

She batted it away and laughed. "He was wonderful." Tara blushed as she described her husband in the jump. He had died in a river accident after they had been married 30 years and had seven grown children.

"He was a good friend and a great leader. I still miss him." I reached across the table and squeezed her hand.

My eyes grazed Trip's face and it was strangely red and his eyes were fiery and intense as he stared across the table at my girlfriend. I glanced at Kate and she was simmering in some kind of physical communication with him, both of their faces flushed with unspoken attraction.

I cast my eyes down, embarrassed to have caught them in such a private moment. I pushed away from the table and noticed Trip moving his legs suddenly. Kate sat up.

"I'm gonna just go rest a bit before we get back to the computers." I murmured and left the room quickly.

I turned the corner and entered the empty boy's room and stood in front of the mirror. "Eye on the prize, Corey. Keep your eye on the prize," I told myself. I was going to keep her alive no matter what the cost.

There was a tiny knock on the door and Kate pushed it open and let herself in. She closed the door behind her and leaned against it as she took in the sight of me. I watched her in the mirror and then turned around. I don't know what she saw in my face, but she ran into my arms.

"Corey! What is wrong?" I sat down on the edge of my bed and she pressed herself against me and kissed my face tenderly. "What is this fearful look in your eyes? I don't like it," she said between kisses.

I gathered her into my arms and we stretched out on the bed. She never stopped kissing my face.

I tucked her under my chin and she wrapped her arms around me. *My Kate! My heart would break it if I lost you to Trip after waiting for you for so long, but even worse, I would die if anything were to happen to you because I closed you away from him.* These were my thoughts, but my words were different.

"Let's get some rest."

"I love you, Corey."

"I know." I lifted her chin and looked into her eyes. "I know," I whispered and kissed her sweet lips, then cradled her to my chest and we slept.

I woke in the middle of the night. Kate stirred in her sleep, apparently having a nightmare. I glanced around the dark room and noted the others had come and found their beds, soft snores and some not so soft rumbled around the dorm room.

Kate squirmed breathing heavily and mumbling, the hall light reflected off of her pale and perfect skin and my heart swelled in my chest at her sweetness. Her brow crinkled and I kissed it. She calmed at my touch and I stroked her cheek until she sighed and snuggled into my chest. I closed my eyes and settled back down when she murmured.

"Trip will save me."

My heart cracked into a million shards.

## BRAN AND BOERNE
### BY JACEN DUDGEON

(LIVELY BAR TUNE)

*Two brothers from a nearby clan as different as can be,*
*One strong and good the other a hoodlum and worldly*
*by those who would deem.*
*Boerne was a codger and lost in his cup near daily as*
*some have been told.*
*While Bran had a quick mind, and eye for the hunt,*
*and heart made of pure gold.*
*They carried on about their ways, daily dabbling done.*
*Bran was productive many good days while Boerne*
*shirked his sunlight on rum.*

*Singing lie lie the merry ol' day. Singing lie lie the*
*merry ol' way.*

*When their father, the king, was old in his days and*
*heard death rattlin' a chain.*
*He called them together, both of them fellers, to choose*
*the son who would reign.*
*The brothers came quickly to sit at his side and be*
*with him, hearts sad and broken.*
*He spoke of their lives with pity and pride and gave*
*them his last words spoken.*
*Bran you have been a model son, good to the core it*
*would seem.*
*But Boerne you have frolicked and danced and*
*cavorted and spent all your days in a dream.*

*Singing lie lie the merry ol' day, singing lie lie the merry ol' way.*

*So Bran became the king of the land, and justice was in his right hand.*
*But Boerne just went on about his shamed ways and became the scoff of the land.*
*So remember this, when a duty you shirk or when choosing where you'll turn up.*
*A price will be paid for cavorting or work, like Bran in his castle and Boerne in his cup*

*Singing lie lie the merry ol' day. Singing lie lie the merry ol' way.*
*Singing lie lie the merry ol' day. Singing lie lie the merry ol' way.*

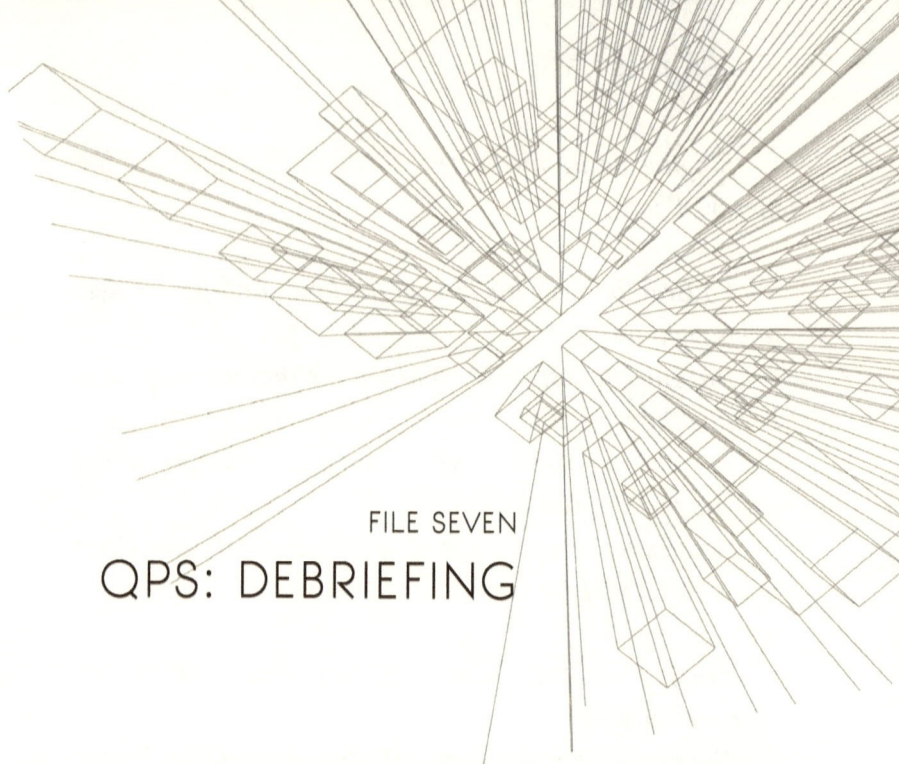

WE SAT IN a large conference room at a table with high back leather chairs pulled up to an oval mahogany table with a marble inset down the center. The dark walls were covered with video projectors, enormous flat screens, and marker boards. Compads rested in front of each of us with black leather covers. Mama Ty sat at one end of the conference table tapping the holo keys of her compad, waiting for everyone to arrive. Dirk drummed his fingers at the opposite end. Kate took my right hand under the table, and Kim shifted in her chair on my left. Tara and Mel sat across from us with their heads together in a whispered conversation. Trip and Donnie hurried in to take their seats across from us.

Mama Ty started the meeting. "This is how it is going to work. We have placed the entire jumper population on infirmary leave. That means none of them are available for jumps, they will be listed as incapacitated for various reasons. They are removed from active status in the system. That way we can activate one extra jumper at a time to go with the task force."

"Is that necessary? Can't just the seven of us go?" Donnie asked.

"The first few jumps we could get away with that, but I am afraid we will alert the infiltrator if we jump only the same seven people. As it is, I am worried they will catch on. As long as we have a new jumper targeted each time, I think the rest of you will go unnoticed."

"So, you are planning on putting a non-task force member with us each time as a target jumper," Tara clarified.

"Yes, I think it will help you get to the issues more quickly if you don't have to decide whose jump you are on each time."

Everyone nodded in agreement. The hardest part of the jump was trying to decide who the target was and help them deal with their issues.

It took me 212 years to finally recognize my jump and even then it took my dying wife to clue me in. When I finally accepted the jump had failed, and we were never going home, I took a permanent position with the Darchori and married the chief's daughter, Taylia. Beautiful Taylia.

Taylia's skin as dark as Kate's was pale, her body voluptuous as Kate's was lithe. Taylia, outspoken and wise, had celebrated thirty five years before we married. We had spent three years as friends. I supported her through the grieving of her first husband, listened to her startling ideas, held her at night when she couldn't sleep. She was a perfect wife, kind and respectful, tending to my every need, except one. Our first kiss was almost comical.

Nothing, no flutters, no emotion, no chemistry, like kissing the wall, we pulled away from one another and laughed. The marriage remained a good arrangement for both of us, though. She didn't have the will to move past the love she had for her first husband, and evidently in that world, I didn't have a heart or soul. Mine had stayed in our world, with Kate. Taylia became the chief of the tribe being married to the Cianti Todura, and I was able to keep the relentless pursuers away because she was my "wife."

We would talk late into the night snuggling, holding hands. Her favorite story was about Kate of a Thousand Years. She said I truly came alive when I spoke of Kate. As she aged our relationship shifted, she became maternal, looking out for my needs and benefits. Later years she confessed that she had one regret.

"I should have made love to you, Corey. I should have made you a father. You would have been the best father a child could imagine."

I kissed her wrinkled forehead and told her our life was perfect. I couldn't bear to tell her I would have never agreed. I only wanted one woman and if someday I had children, I wanted them to come from her. My Kate.

"I'm dying, Corey. You know this better than anyone," she told me one night as she stroked my cheek.

"No, Taylia, I can't bear it."

"Corey, husband, I ask one promise of you."

"Anything, my friend." I pressed the back of her frail hand to my lips, fighting tears.

"Never give up on Kate. She will come for you. I am sure of it. A woman so loved by a man like you could never give up on him. She will come."

"I promise, Taylia. I believe it. My Kate will come."

Taylia lived to see it. Kate walked up to her, holding my hand, and hugged Taylia like a dear friend. Taylia's eyes shone with rapturous joy as she eyed me over Kate's embrace. The greatest wish of her life was to see Kate of a Thousand Years reunited with her true love.

On the platform when Kate and I were so enmeshed with one another, ready to become husband and wife, Taylia's joy beamed, tangible. When I saw her reaction to the undeniable and fervent love between Kate and me, something shifted in her. Her will to stay faded from her face.

My heart ached.

When Kate told me to take my wife home, I was almost relieved—almost. I carried her home, tucked her into bed and she pulled me alongside her.

"I am complete."

I drew the coverlet around her shoulders and settled beside her.

"Birsharon will be an excellent leader. She already does most of the work," her frail voice whispered into the night. "You have chosen your successor well, too, my husband. I believe Whelshti will make an excellent Cianti Todura."

I nodded and tucked her head against my chest. The ache in my chest wouldn't abide any distance between us tonight. I let the tears flow as she spoke her goodbyes in words of gratitude and contentment.

She slept soundly in my arms. I stayed awake with her all night, afraid she would drift off to the final sleep without me beside her. I stayed with my life companion and ruminated on the good life we had built together.

Before the sunrise, as the Tondo rose from the gardens in their morning flurry of wings and croons, Taylia woke and asked for her servant.

"Go get Kate and Eunavae and bring them to me," her frail voice whispered. "Your lives together are going to start today."

She was right. The sphere came for us at the moment of Taylia's death. My grief and joy were so intermingled that it created a heightened emotional state that Kate and I could not resist. We were powerless against our feelings for one another. I had not felt physical attraction for two hundred years. With Kate in my arms electricity shot through me and I needed to pour into her two centuries of affection.

Her receptivity staggered me and increased my longing for her. I would have taken her as my wife under that willow tree, if we hadn't been interrupted. It was time. I had waited long enough. We both wanted it, needed it, ran toward it with abandon.

I think if we had been able to complete our union that night, Kate would not have fluctuated in her feelings. Things changed after that.

The task force was formed and now we found ourselves in the dank basement facility of the Inner Circle, planning to jump into the unknown with Kate, basically, as the bait.

I hated the plan, but knew it was the only chance to save the technology that my great great grandfather Dr. Rick Wilson invented from evil intent. If she was going to survive this quest, I needed Trip to bind himself to her and move heaven and hell to save her. It broke my heart every time they would saunter off. I felt every kiss I imagined they shared in the pit of my being. Every touch, every passionate look that passed between them, was a knife coring out a hollow in me, but I kept my focus on the prize—keeping Kate alive. I was confident that between Trip and me, we could protect her.

Mama Ty continued speaking. I jerked my attention back to the debriefing. "We are only going to add jumpers from the Chartreuse team right now. They are adults, really, after that two century jump, and their longevity will prepare them emotionally to handle the situations better."

"Aren't they emotionally strained enough as it is?" Mel interjected.

"They have been resilient," Kim stated, she had come back early this morning bearing Krispy Kremes that Trip was busy finishing off at the moment. "Most of them are good to go. I think we need to give Caitlyn and Navarro a bit more time. Honestly, I don't know if you will be able to separate them long enough for one to jump without the other."

"Kim will coordinate the jumpers camp side, and arrange errands and other timely favors that will send one of them to your cabin." Mama Ty tapped her Compad and a map of the campus popped up over Dirk's head.

For a full-sized, color map of Heartwork Village, visit
www.ladonnacolern.wix.com/ladonna-cole

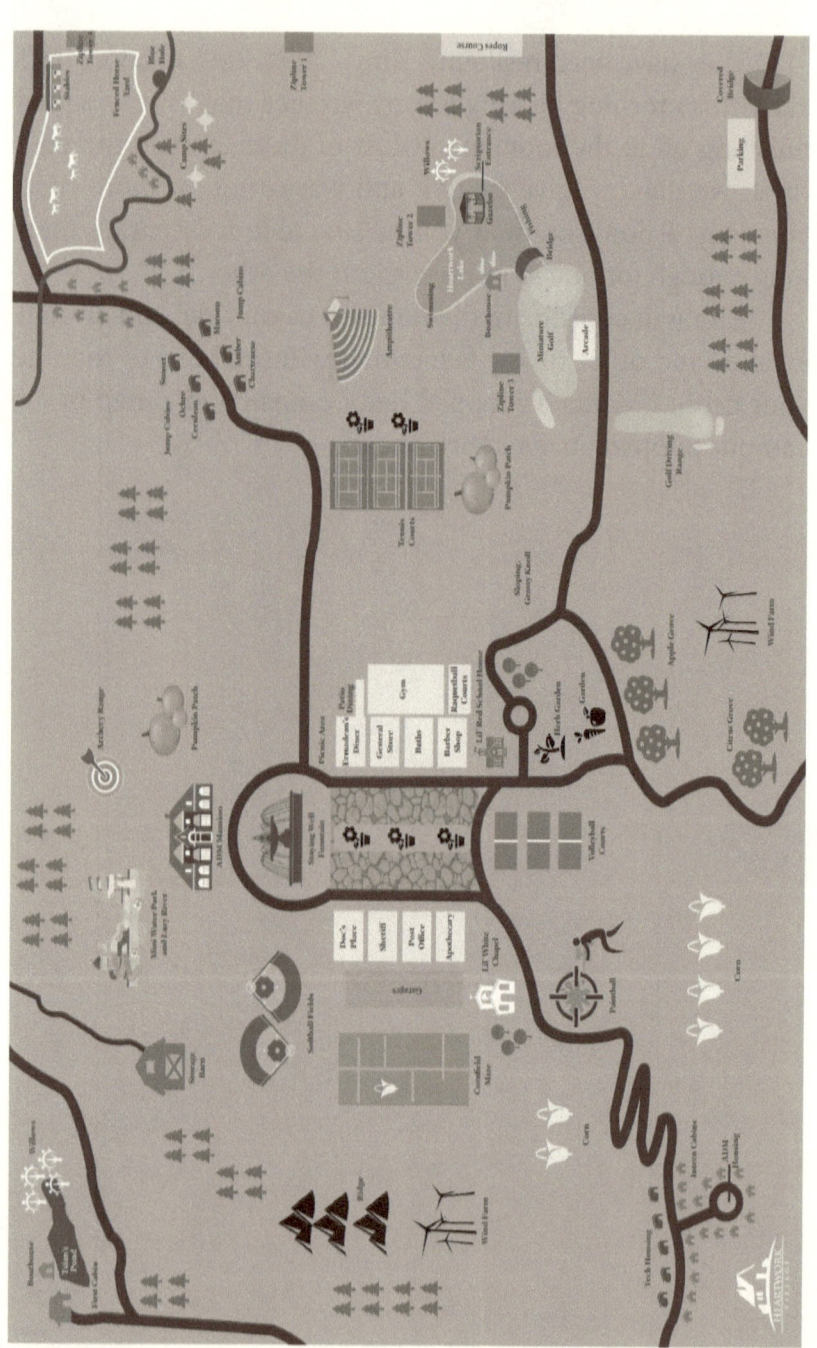

"After your training here, you will all be relocated to First Cabin. It is more remote, set apart from the rest of the village. When you aren't on a jump, you will stay there. There is an apartment above the boat house for the old married couple." She smiled at Mel and Donnie. "The rest of you can stay in the cabin."

Donnie grinned at Mel and I admit I felt a bit jealous. If Kate had been with us on that long jump, we would have probably been married by now, too. I wondered if Tara thought the same thing about Trip. I glanced at him. He was smiling at Kate, suggestively. I turned to look at her and she rolled her eyes at him, but the blush in her cheeks spoke volumes.

I snapped my eyes away for a distraction and landed on the picture of First Cabin. It had a wide front porch opening to a green lawn that swooped down to a small pond. That pond had been the site of the very first jump. My great great grandmother had been taken to a land called Ampeliagia at that very lake. Then years later, my own grandmother had crossed into Ampeliagia and come back within hours.

It was her disappearance that caused her grandfather, Rick Wilson, to develop the original sphere matrix. It had taken 40 years to actually put the algorithm into practice. Rick was long in his grave by the time the first sphere was deemed stable enough for transport. The technology had come a long way since then.

I felt a strange connection to the cabin as I stared at the picture. I would probably settle down there one day and raise a family. I glanced at Kate and prayed that she would be by my side when I did.

Mama Ty had continued the debriefing. "...Mel's organizational expertise."

Mel chimed in. "Get me a list of your favorite foods so we will be stocked and ready."

Dirk spoke up. "We aren't going to have to worry about shelter and protection either. We will be fully packed and armed." He stroked his Compad and the monitor over his head popped up. "These are the weapons that will go through the quantum stream without disruption. Each of you should choose one and become proficient with it over the next three weeks."

He looked at Donnie who jerked up and cleared his throat. "I have programmed tutorials on the G drive for each of these weapons, and Trip and Tara are trained in most of them. They will conduct the training sessions."

"We have this cool simulation chamber that has several scenarios programmed into it. It's pretty much like arena training except in a safe environment." Trip seemed excited about weapons training. I looked forward to training with him.

"Kate and Corey," Mama Ty addressed us. "Dirk tells me you have hit a wall with the information in our systems on your security level. I will immediately remove all security constraints and give you full clearance. I can't believe I didn't do that sooner."

I frowned at her. I didn't want her to say any more about my clearance status. I didn't want anyone to know just yet what my connection was to the village. I felt it was beneficial to the mission that I just be Corey, friend, team member, advisor, spiritual mentor, and boyfriend.

Boyfriend, hmm that didn't sound quite right. Kate felt much more important to me than that title described.

"Study the profiles carefully. We have had extensive psychological, emotional, and spiritual profiles done on each member of the Inner Circle. You should have everything you need in these files." She tapped her Compad and a few seconds later mine and Kate's Compads registered an item in our inboxes.

"We have designated this team as 'The Keepers.'" She pinned Tara with a mischievous smile. "To solve the problem of duplicate names. Kim's cabin will retain the name Chartreuse team."

Kate cleared her throat. "Excuse me, Mama Ty." Her voice was nearly a whisper.

"Yes."

"You keep saying we." Kate glanced around the room. "Who else knows about our task force?"

"No one outside of this room knows the actual purpose behind this task force. I have told the staff and board that you have been selected for early jump leader training, and that is true. I will be making a full report to the board at the end of your training."

"Speaking of which." Donnie tapped his compad. "I have taken the liberty of modifying the training material to fit our schedules."

A graph loaded onto the flat screen and our compads.

| | Monday | Tuesday | Wednesday | Thursday | Friday | Saturday | Sunday |
|---|---|---|---|---|---|---|---|
| 8-12 | Dirk Team Building | Melanie Leadership Workshop | Donnie Buckets, Balls, Balance | Corey First Aid Quantum Theory | Guest Speaker Scientists, Psych Professionals | Crisis Intervention CPI | Group Actives |
| 12-1 | Lunch Lecture | Lunch Lecture | Lunch Lecture | Lunch Lecture | Lunch Lecture | | |
| 1-3 | Corey and Kate Research / Dirk, Mel, Donnie Weapons | Corey and Kate Research / Dirk, Mel, Donnie Weapons | Corey and Kate Research / Dirk, Mel, Donnie Weapons | Corey and Kate Research / Dirk, Mel, Donnie Weapons | Corey and Kate Research / Dirk, Mel, Donnie Weapons | Mel-Psychology of Jumps / Trust Exercise | Ropes |
| 3-5 | Corey, Kate Weapons / Dirk, Mel, Donnie Lesson Plans | Corey, Kate Weapons / Dirk, Mel, Donnie Lesson Plans | Corey, Kate Weapons / Dirk, Mel, Donnie Lesson Plans | Corey, Kate Weapons / Dirk, Mel, Donnie Lesson Plans | Corey, Kate Weapons / Dirk, Mel, Donnie Lesson Plans | Dirk-HWV Curriculum / Donnie-Tech Talk, Equipment Management | Herbs, medicinals and Extrateran Plant Life |
| 6p | Dinner Debrief | Dinner Debrief | Dinner Debrief | Dinner Debrief | Dinner Debrief | Dinner | Dinner |
| 7-9 | Free/Kate | Free/Kate | Free/Kate | Free/Kate | Free/Kate | Free | Free |

Week one Training will focus on Theory. Week two will focus on Practical Application. Week three will focus on Train the Trainer and Practical Leadership in each topic.

"Sounds grueling," Tara interjected. I had known her long enough to recognize the sarcasm. I also remembered the 16 hour training days she put the warriors of Jewel City through. I cracked a smile in her direction.

"After three weeks of training, we will relocate to First Cabin and start the jumps," Dirk finished.

"We will get another Scriptorium excursion, right?" I asked.

"Yes, the last day of training we will take you back to the Village and to the Scriptorium."

I glanced at Kate. The blush in her cheeks and simmering eyes took me back to our pink clouds and thousand years in our Scriptorium experience. I squeezed her hand to let her know I was right there in those pink clouds with her.

*Sigh.* My Kate.

"Family week is the next week, Mama Ty. Their parents and families will be here." Kim stated and tapped the calendar on her compad.

"True, all jumps are suspended during family week, so you will have some time to settle into First Cabin before you are launched into this assignment." Mama Ty paused and took an urgent message.

We broke into separate conversations while she dealt with some administrative issue. She finished and called the meeting back to order.

"Your morning training will be intense and heart scathing. I expect you to give it one hundred percent of your efforts. It could very well be the thing that makes or breaks this quest."

I studied the schedule, a lot to learn in three weeks. Would we be ready?

# QPS: PREPARATION

"COREY, I WONDER how big is this place?" Kate pressed into my side to look around me down the endless maze of intersecting halls as we slowly ambled through the corridor.

"Seems massive, doesn't it?" The warmth of her arm pressed against mine sent waves of euphoria through me and once again I was caught up in the overwhelming attraction of Kate Wilson.

Our eyes met and I was home. This girl was everything to me, my hopes, my dreams, my desires, my purpose. My Kate.

She glanced at me, flashed a smile, and then sobered at something she saw in my face. Her eyes simmered with emotion. She drifted closer to me. Like a magnet, I drew her. The intensity of our attraction ricocheted between us. It gave me deep satisfaction that she felt the staggering connection too.

"We should go in, yes?" Her soft voice quivered as she hooked a thumb toward the combat training center.

"Yeah, we should." We stood toe to toe, pressing our palms and lacing our fingers together as we grinned and stalled for a few more seconds alone.

I reluctantly reached behind her for the doorknob and lifted her over the threshold brushing her forehead with a kiss. She giggled when I set her down and we turned toward the training room.

We stepped into a Roman coliseum. Ancient ruins encircled a sand covered arena. We gawked at the extremely realistic holo-projection.

Trip and Tara sauntered up to us in their black belted karate gi and grinned.

"Wow!" Kate breathed.

"I'll second that," I muttered and scanned the circumference of the massive pavilion.

"We programmed the quantum replicating algorithm to create this room from our memories of our Scriptorium training." Tara spread her arms and turned in a circle.

"We can make it into anything we can imagine," Trip stated, twirling a short sword between his fingers. "Or, I should say, the white coats can."

"Like in my jump?" Kate asked, a crease forming between her brows.

"No." Tara touched her arm. "This place cannot read your thoughts. We have to manually input changes."

Kate's shoulders returned to a relaxed state.

"So, where do we start?"

"I have something for you." Tara took me by the arm and dragged me over to the wall of weapons. "Remember this?"

She slipped a golden short sword out of a sheath and turned the handle toward me. The hilt was etched with the image of intertwining serpents with emeralds for eyes. They spiraled around the pommel up to the cross beam in an elaborate caduceus-like design. The blade was etched with indecipherable glyphs.

"That's the dagger from my pack." I examined the hilt closely. "Did you take it?"

"Nope, all of these weapons were here when Trip and I got here this morning." She waved her arm at the wall of weapons. "I thought you would want it back. It's called a Gladius, It's Roman. Did you know that?"

"Gladius, huh?" I cut a figure eight, testing the weight of it, remembering the feel of it in my hand. "It's been awhile." It did seem to blend perfectly with this room.

Tara pinned me with her stoic eyes.

"What?"

"Do you think we will be ready?"

I dropped my sword arm and stepped closer to her. "What's wrong, Tara?" I knew her better than most. She never showed her emotions, keeping them hidden behind a warrior's mask. For her to even ask the question meant she was worried.

"This assignment, the team, everything."

Tara was worried that we wouldn't be prepared. "Who exactly are you concerned about, Tara?"

"Mel and Donnie are fine, they have years of experience. Dirk too." She ground her teeth together and cut her eyes across the room.

"That just leaves me and Kate." An expression of deep sorrow flashed through her eyes so quickly I would have missed it if I hadn't been studying her face. I turned to see what she was distracted by and noticed Kate and Trip deep in the middle of a martial arts lesson. Trip was guiding Kate's arms and legs into various positions.

"Are you worried about Kate?" I asked. Friction defined Tara and Kate's relationship, from our very first jump together to the dragon world where Kate had been captured by a colony of dragons and enslaved to be The Mother.

"Are you, Tara?" I asked again. "Do you think Kate can't handle it?"

She snapped her eyes to mine and shook her head. "It doesn't matter. She is important to the quest. I am just worried that you and Trip will be at risk protecting her." She smirked at me. "I guess I will just have to guard both of your backs."

I chortled. "You can protect my back any time, my friend. I couldn't have a better champion."

She beamed at me and picked up a sword. "Well, looks like you're stuck with me. They are well into a lesson, and we are falling behind." She flourished her weapon. "Like old times, right Old Man?"

"You aren't gonna take it easy on me are you?"

"Nope!" She popped the "p" and lunged at me.

I had sparred with Tara for decades in our two century jump, but was out of practice since my last 50 years were with the peace loving Darchori, so I was very rusty and she pressed her full advantage. After she disarmed me for the seventh time and I found myself on my back side staring up into her beautifully frightening battle glow, I threw up my hands.

"Mercy!" I called, hands in the air, sweat streaming down my face into my eyes as I panted for breath.

"You know, not too bad for an old man." She laughed and stretched out her hand to help me up.

"You are as old as I am." I grumbled. Being over two hundred years old and stuck in a teenager's body again took some adjustment. At first it was invigorating, returning back to a young ache-free version of myself. But the wild emotions and intensity took every ounce of control I'd learned.

We glanced over to Kate and Trip. They had ended up on the floor in one of their combat moves. Kate was stretched out on top of Trip and they were frozen, gazing heatedly into one another's eyes.

Tara whisked away, stalked to the weapons rack, and slammed her sword down with a crash. Trip and Kate splintered apart with flushed faces. Kate scrambled up and glanced at me, worry drenched her eyes and she pressed her palms together.

I shoved my pain down deep inside and smiled back reassuringly. She took a shuddering breath and walked over to me without looking back at Trip. I opened my arms and she melted into them and pressed into my chest. I enfolded her in a hug while watching Trip over her head. He was still seated on the ground where she left him staring at the back wall.

Complicated.

"So are you a certified black belt yet?" I tilted Kate's chin up to gaze into her face.

"On my way," she grinned. "Have you chosen the short sword as your weapon?" She pointed at the weapon in my hand.

"Well, I thought it was a good choice since there was one in my pack. I am obviously going to have to use it."

She arched a brow in contemplation and nodded, then subtly cut her eyes over to Trip. "I guess I should choose a weapon, huh?"

She sashayed over to Tara, and they began discussing her options. I crossed the arena floor to Trip. "Teach me some moves, bro."

He cocked his head, our eyes met, and I tried to give him an expression of understanding. I knew how he felt about my girlfriend and needed him to know I had no malice.

Trip nodded. "I will teach you the way I was taught. We don't have time to go through different katas. You are going to have to learn the arena method, fast and deadly, but if you ever do take Karate or martial arts, you will have to start from scratch."

I nodded. I knew where I would have to start. It wasn't scratch. One of the benefits of being from a wealthy family whose parents were preoccupied was endless lessons. I spent most of my afternoons during the school year in the limo with Giles, riding from lesson to lesson. The summers were full of karate camp, fencing lessons, Taekwondo, music lessons, you name it, my parents paid for it. I was a second level black belt, but that was over 212 years ago. I didn't have any current skills and didn't know how long it would take to regain them.

"Well, show me what you've got," I said.

He took me through the basic steps, kicks, and punches in slow deliberate moves, then said, "Okay, come at me." He shifted one foot back and snapped into a defensive posture.

I took a deep breath. Trip and I were about the same height, but where I was lean, he was massive, where I was quick, he was strong. This was going to be interesting. I had one chance to beat him at his own game, and once he knew my skills, I would never get the element of surprise back.

I held nothing back. I launched at him at full speed and just before I got to him, executed an aerial flip, landed behind him and jabbed the back of his knees. He went down, rolled over, but I was on him like lightning. I checked my punches so I wouldn't harm him, but landed five blows to the chest before he recovered from his shock and slammed me to the ground.

My lungs seized up and I couldn't breathe. I rolled to my side and waited for them to work again. Gazing at me with a crooked smile on his face, he squatted down beside me.

"You've been holding out," he chuckled.

I tried to smile back but still couldn't breathe, so I just nodded.

"I knew you had it in you."

My lungs finally released and I gulped in much coveted air. He offered me his hand, I took it, and he lifted me off the ground.

I turned to look at the girls. Tara had her arms crossed in front of her with a satisfied smile, she had seen me fight many times over the years. We had traded moves and I had even taught some of my skills to her students. Kate held her head at an angle with her lips pursed and brow creased as though she couldn't quite make out what had happened.

Then her whole demeanor shifted. She glanced at Trip, studied me, then turned to study Tara and a fierce determination dawned over her features. She stood up straight, grasped the whip with both hands, and cocked an eyebrow at me.

I chuckled. I couldn't wait to talk to her and find out what was going through that amazing head of hers.

Now that Trip knew my skills, he advanced my training considerably. We were doing some pretty high level maneuvers by the end of the day. The girls had finished before us and Trip and I rambled into the boy's dorms to shower before dinner.

"Corey." Trip tossed me a towel. "It is good to have another warrior on our team."

I gave him a nod and stepped into the hall toward the showers.

# TARA AND HER MIGHTY BAND
## BY COREY CHASTAIN

*A maiden fair of steel strength and air,*
*Came to stand on Mountain land*
*In the fairest city of all.*

*A war-maid strong, her spear-throw long*
*Gave to all a battle call.*
*The bravest one of all.*

*Tara and her mighty band*
*Tara and her mighty band*
*Tara and her mighty band of warriors.*

*The young men showed to test her bold*
*Raised a band of fighters and*
*Tried to best her one and all.*

*Her moves were right, gave them a fright*
*None could match her steady snatch*
*The best warrior of them all.*

*Tara and her mighty band*
*Tara and her mighty band*
*Tara and her mighty band of warriors.*

*Her battle glow was fierce to know.*
*No man withstood, nor ever could.*
*The war maven felled them all.*

*They begged her to teach them new*
*Ways to kill, increase their skill*
*Make them the best war band of them all.*

*Tara and her mighty band*
*Tara and her mighty band*
*Tara and her mighty band of warriors.*

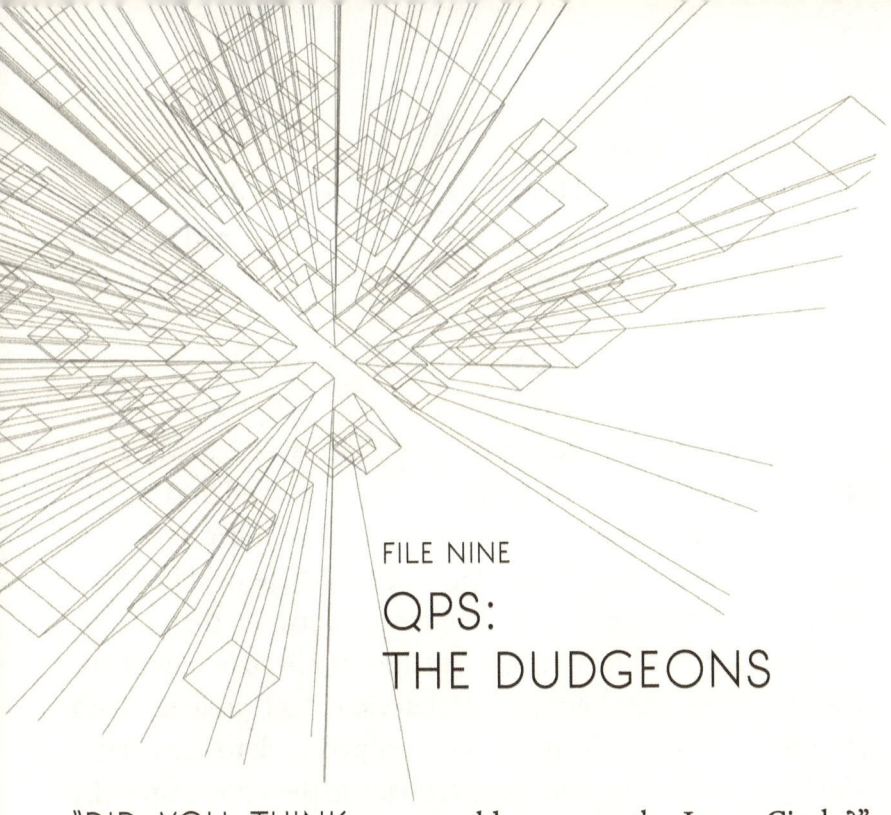

FILE NINE
# QPS:
# THE DUDGEONS

"DID YOU THINK we would ever see the Inner Circle?" Donnie crossed his arms and leaned back in his chair. The compad in front of him blinked off.

"No way," Mel answered from her desk behind him. "I've been coming here for almost ten earth years and I didn't even know an Inner Circle existed until a couple of years ago."

"Top Secret stuff, for sure."

"Jacen would love this wouldn't he?" Mel took a deep breath and sighed.

Donnie chuckled. His youngest son in Jewel City was a rambunctious little thing that roamed the mountains looking for mystery and intrigue. "Yeah. He was born into the wrong world for sure. He'd have loved spy novels and super heroes here."

They turned to each other and pretended they were peering around a tree, clandestinely. Mimicking their son's daily behavior back in Jewel City, Mel grinned and Donnie snorted, then they turned around to their comp stations again and worked in silence for a few moments.

"I wonder how old he is now," Mel whispered.

Donnie heard the sorrow in her voice and turned his chair around to face her. "Hey." He maneuvered her around and took her hands.

Her chin quivered and she lifted her face to his.

"Babe, it's okay. I miss them too."

She nodded. "There are days I think I will die. My arms ache to hold them." She left her chair and crawled into his lap.

Donnie gathered his wife into his arms and pressed his chin to the top of her head. "I know, babe." He held her for a few minutes and they shared the burden between them.

Two hundred and twelve years they had lived in Jewel City. They had raised 68 children over that time. Mel, pregnant with their 69th, lost the baby when they jumped back to the village. The DNA replicators reset jumpers back to their prejump DNA pattern when they returned to home dimension (Earth) in the Quantum Home Room. Mel had not been pregnant going into the two century jump, so she reset to that physical state. It was supposed to protect the jumpers from bringing home disease and injury obtained in the alternate realities. Also, they weren't supposed to be in those realities for more than a few hours. When things started to go wrong, those security measures ceased to protect and became a source of great pain and anguish.

Devastated and 20 years young again, Donnie and Mel chose to remain married in home dimension too. Kids were definitely in the future, but Mel wanted them both to finish college and work the village a few more years before they settled down.

Donnie agreed, though he loved being a dad and wouldn't mind if they started to work right away on their next 68 kids. Mel shut him down pretty quick when he mentioned it to her.

"Three, tops!" she'd insisted.

Mel took a deep, shuddering breath, kissed Donnie on the cheek, and said. "Thanks, Babe."

He hugged her again before she returned to her own chair. "My lesson plan is almost done. Yours?"

Mel typed a few more words into the compad holo keyboard, then swiped her hand over the projection. It recorded her thumb print, saved the document, and shut down. "Done!"

"We've got about an hour before dinner. What do you want to do with our free time Mrs. Dudgeon?" He nuzzled into her neck.

Mel laughed. "Not that, Mr. Dudgeon!" She stood and stretched. "Let's walk to the atrium and talk shop."

Donnie followed her, grumbling. "I miss Jewel City and our big house on top of the mountain."

Mel cut her eyes at him. "Don't you mean you miss our private bedroom inside of the big house on top of the mountain in Jewel City?"

"Yeah. That." He tucked her under his arm as they moved into the hall and started toward the center of the underground facility.

"Poor you," she said with little sympathy and poked him in the ribs. "Hang in there, Babe, only a few more days and we'll have our very own boathouse."

"Ouch!" He rubbed at his rib, then flung sarcasm at her. "Can't wait, if that's the treatment I'll get," he teased.

They turned down several long corridors. Mel lapsed into deep thought, gnawing on her thumbnail. Donnie walked alongside her in silence, watching her grow anxious as she contemplated something.

The last hallway opened into a large commons area with a vaulted ceiling and a fountain that shot into the heights of the ceiling, then tumbled to splash into the circular pool surrounding it. Planters were strategically placed around the area to give it a park feeling. Though how they grew in fluorescent lighting, Donnie had no clue.

They started a lap around the fountain before Donnie broke into Mel's reverie. "Melanie, you're gnawing that thumbnail to the bone. Talk."

"What?" She pulled the thumb away from her teeth and frowned. "Ugh! You're supposed to stop me from doing that," she groused.

"You were engrossed. I didn't want to disturb you." Donnie pulled her over to a park bench and sat her down. "What are you thinking?"

"Just thinking about how all the safety protocols have failed and what that could potentially mean."

"What specifically?"

"We could get stuck in another dimension, Donnie. We might be separated from our families." She snapped her eyes to him. "Well, I mean my family. Sorry."

"Your family is practically mine, Mel," he said softly.

"Right! What if we got stuck somewhere for thousands of years? What if we died there? What if time accelerated here and they all got old and died while we were in a jump?" Her thumbnail snuck between her incisors.

Donnie gently reached up and took her hand between his. She made a guilty face and clasped her hands together in his.

"You've been jumping a long time, Mel. You've always known these were possibilities."

"Yeah, but that was before the safety protocols malfunctioned." Her voice lowered to a whisper. "Before we lost everyone in Jewel City." She stared ahead at the fountain, lost in memories.

"Are you sure you are ready to do this? We are going to be in danger all the time. I'm sure Mama Ty would give you a leave of absence."

"No!" she cried. "You go, I go. Period." She pierced him with a stern gaze. "Got it. I'm not losing you, too."

Donnie intercepted the fierceness and fervor of her insistence. "Got it." He squeezed her hand.

She nodded once and turned back to the fountain. "Good."

DONNIE AND DIRK slept soundly in the bunks above us. Trip lay on his back on the bottom bunk at my head.

"Are you sure about this, Corey?" he spoke into the darkness in a hushed voice.

"What?"

"This whole thing with Kate."

"Are you talking about our agreement to keep her safe?" Trip and I had agreed on a plan of action. In order to figure out which Inner Circle member was causing all of this trouble, we had to go into the jumps and try to discern who the saboteur was. Because Kate had an uncanny sense of figuring out things in the jumps, we knew she would be in particular danger if the saboteur realized her skill. Trip and I agreed that was enough for her to worry about. We wanted her to feel free to become as close as she needed to every team member, so her intuition would be heightened. It was our way of protecting the team. Keep Kate safe and the team had a better chance of survival.

"Yeah. And..." he paused. "You know, her getting close to all of us?"

I stilled at the tone in his voice. Not exactly sure what he questioned, I waited.

"You know, her getting closer to me?"

"Why are you asking, Trip?"

"Well, you know we were kinda on a path to being together before your Scriptorium. I just think there is some unfinished business between us, you know?"

I sensed we treaded on thin ice. The wrong thing said here could cause a rift in the team before we ever got started.

"Can you tell me what you're feeling, exactly?"

"I don't know. It's pretty personal. I don't really go for the touchy feely conversations, you know? Heh," he laughed nervously.

"Yeah, but you brought it up, so what is it you want to say?"

"I just feel kinda weird is all, getting closer to another guy's girlfriend."

"Well, I'm pretty close to your girlfriend, you know."

"Ain't that the truth," he huffed. "Can't really get much closer than a 200 year relationship, right?"

"Technically, I was with Tara and the team for a hundred and sixty two years. Eunavae was with me the other fifty."

"Jeez, I can't even wrap my brain around that Corey."

"Well, if you think that is close, try spending a thousand years with the girl of your dreams and come out of that with any type of realistic insecurity."

It was his turn to be silent. It took him so long to respond, I thought he had fallen asleep. He finally rolled over and put his chin over his crossed arms. I wrenched my neck up to look at him.

"You aren't worried at all are you? You are solid in your destiny to end up together."

"Yeah, Trip. I am."

"So you don't think she has any feelings for me? In that way, I mean."

"I think Kate has a never ending potential for love. She loves unconditionally and without reservation. I know she loves you. But it doesn't change anything. Our time together and connection puts me at a great advantage. I'm not overly worried about who else she loves." Overly being the operative word, but I didn't say that to Trip.

"You really are an arrogant ass, you know that?" Trip laughed.

"So your girlfriend loves to remind me." I smiled into the darkness and rolled into my blanket thinking of all the times Tara and I had said those words to each other.

Trip fell silent again. Dirk rolled over and the bunk creaked.

Trip whispered into the night. "I swear I will do everything in my power to protect her, Corey."

"I know you will, Trip. I trust you to put her safety above all else. I'm glad you are on this team. We couldn't do it without you."

"Me? What about you and your secret Ninja moves?" he teased.

I popped him in the head with a pillow. "Go to sleep."

He took my pillow and shoved it under his head as he rolled over. "G'night."

This night stood out as a defining moment in our friendship. Somehow just talking about it, getting it out on the table eased the tension between us. Over the next three weeks, we had many late night talks and solidified our plan to keep Kate and the others safe. By the end of our training, Trip, Dirk, and of course Donnie, became my best friends. I'd never trusted a group of guys as much as I trusted them. We trained side by side, day after day, and formed a bond like I imagined brothers had. Even the Jewel City Clan paled in comparison. We'd been focused on survival there. Here we focused on pushing one another to become the tightest and most skilled team imaginable. We each shared our skills to train the others.

Kate spent individual time with each of us and we opened up to her in ways that we'd never opened to anyone before. She became the keeper of all our secrets, wishes, hopes and prayers, until she knew each of us better than we knew ourselves.

It was a grueling pace. During our "free time" Kate insisted on working with her whip or combing through the files. We had everything memorized about each of the Inner Circle members, so I wasn't sure what she was looking for exactly.

"Kate, you know these files forward and backward. Why are you still digging through them?"

She slid her compad onto the table beside her. "I don't know." She started chewing on her lip nervously and I could see her mental gears clicking away.

"Let's take a walk. You can talk it through and maybe come to some answers." I took her hand, pulled her up, tucking her under my arm.

We sauntered blindly without a goal through the corridors, arm in arm.

"There is something more, Corey." She glanced at me. "I know we are missing something. I can't put my finger on it."

"Are you feeling something?"

"No, that's just it. I don't 'feel' like I know them. I should, we have studied every detail of their lives, but the Inner Circle are still strangers."

"Maybe it's time to meet them." I stopped suddenly. "Let's go."

"What? Go? To the Inner Circle?" Kate questioned me as I dragged her down the hall.

"Why not? We have security clearance. Let's use it."

We moved quickly, I didn't want to talk myself out of it. I found the corridor that led to the inner chamber, we swiped our id cards, and the door opened. "That seemed a bit easy."

"Well, we already came through 3 or 4 levels of security with Mama Ty."

"Yeah."

We walked into the chamber, the antiseptic smell burning my nose. Monitors hummed and beeped, accompaniment to the medics weaving in between the beds. One of them looked up at us, startled.

"Are you sure you are supposed to be here, Mr. Chastain?" the head medic asked.

I just cocked an eyebrow at him. He took a step back and held up a palm in apology.

Kate furrowed her brow at the exchange and cut me a questioning glance. I urged her over to the first bed. We looked down into the peaceful face of Reverend Liz Robertson, Phd. The facts on her dossier ran through my brain. American, lives in L.A., highly acclaimed faith healer, author, and prophetess. She served as the spiritual link in the Inner Circle.

"Hello Dr. Robertson." Kate touched her hand. "I am Kate Wilson." She stood there with her eyes closed, listening, feeling. I don't know what she was doing, exactly. After a few moments she opened her eyes and scanned the body in front of her, searching, memorizing. We moved to the next person.

"Dr. Akio Fujitani, of Kyoto, Japan," I quoted his dossier from memory. "Specializes in Extraterrestrial tectonics and Atmoshperic Physics. Geophysicist and Meteorologist."

Kate didn't seem to hear me. She just stood at his side with eyes closed and rested her hand on his arm. She did same with all twelve of the Inner Circle members. When we would leave one, the medics would close in behind us and continue their ministrations.

"Dr. Gregorvitch Mattovdzky, PhD, Quantum Mechanics," she whispered as we drew up beside the last bed. Kate snapped her eyes open and turned her head to make eye contact with one of the medics, an exotic dark skinned woman with large soulful eyes. She reminded me a bit of Taylia, my Darchori wife. They peered into one another's eyes in some silent communication, then the medic smiled at Kate. She nodded and we exited.

"Well?" I asked.

"Hmmm." She was pensive as we strolled back to our side of the facility. "Yeah, I think that was what I needed." She simmered into my eyes. "Thank you, Corey." Kate squeezed my hand.

"Now, can I have a few moments of your attention, Kate Wilson?" I slipped into an alcove in the hallway and welcomed her into my arms.

"Have I been neglecting you, my Corey?" She pressed her body against mine and wrapped her arms around my neck.

"No, just preoccupied."

"I can fix that." She lifted her face and her eyes were full of longing and love.

The familiar tension ricocheted between us and suddenly I was back on the platform in the Darchori night sky with the huge silver moon as our back drop, Kate in my arms, finally. "My Kate," I whispered and closed the distance to her lips.

The kiss was so powerful that we fell against the corridor wall. She wrapped her legs around me and I lifted her into my arms and burned for her. Our kisses became urgent. We hadn't ignited to this degree since the night under the willow tree, when we were interrupted.

I ran my hands down her back found the skin where her shirt separated from her jeans and felt her passion spike. She moaned and it nearly drove me insane. I couldn't get enough of this beautiful, desirable girl in my arms. I carried her into an empty office that was shut down for the night and we stretched out on the couch and continued our make-up-for-lost-time kisses.

Tomorrow we would move back to the campus, descend into the Scriptorium, and our lives would change forever. Tonight was ours and we spent the whole of it in our favorite activity, kissing, talking, floating on the memories of pink clouds and eternal love.

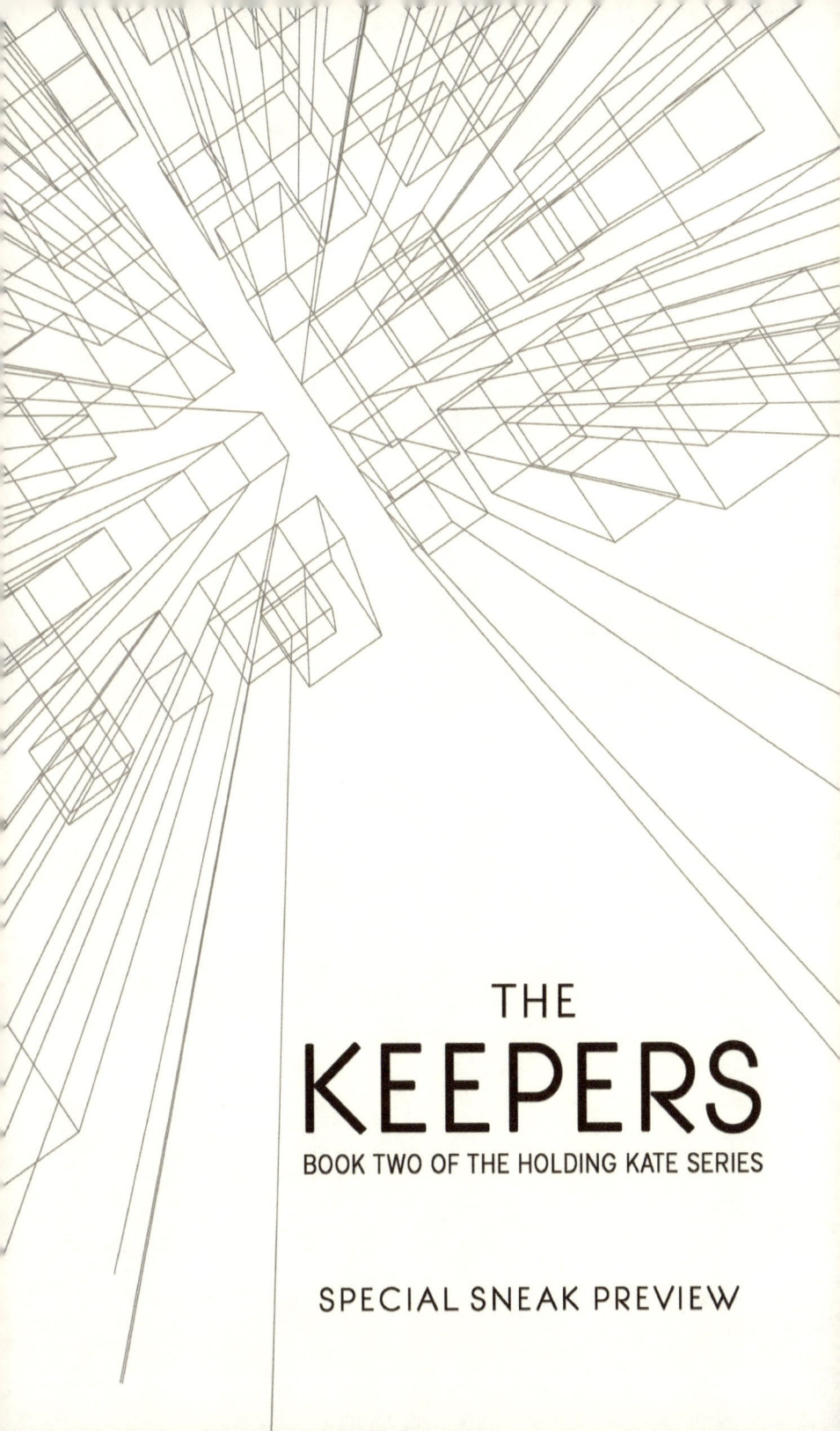

# THE
# KEEPERS
## BOOK TWO OF THE HOLDING KATE SERIES

### SPECIAL SNEAK PREVIEW

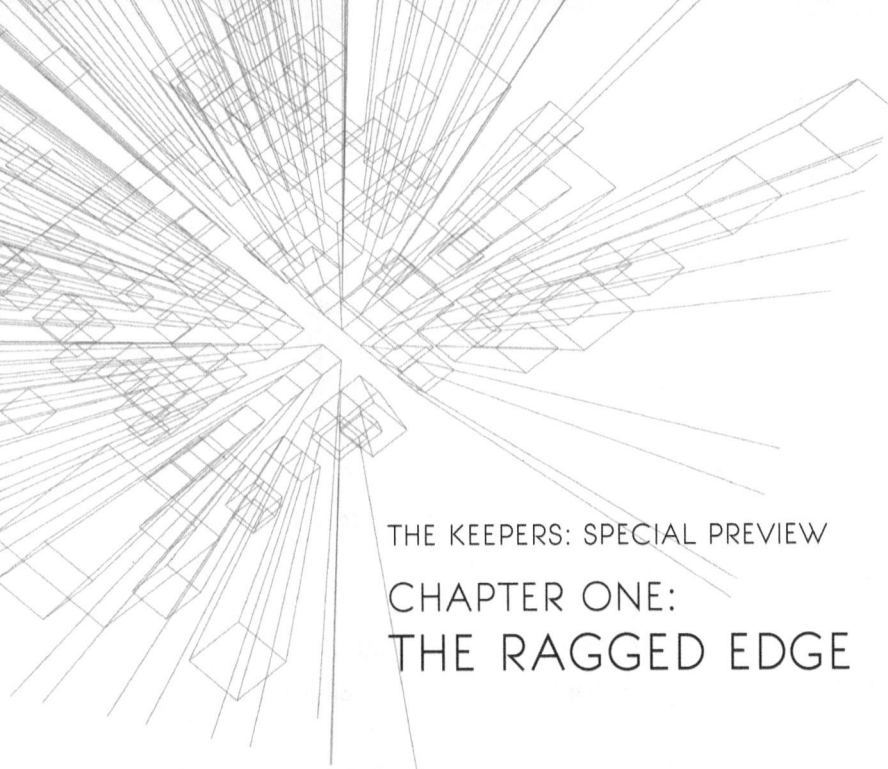

# CHAPTER ONE:
# THE RAGGED EDGE

*"Through the discovery of intellectual streaming of Quantum Mechanics, we have perfected the interactive matrix linking individual imagination to a hive imagination to produce creative molecular cohesion."* ~ **Dr. K. Pazicni**, December 2022

THE VAN LURCHED to a stop. I eased the blindfold over my right eye, then took it off. The old covered bridge stood near the parking lot where we sat. I took Kate's blindfold off and opened the door. Seven of us poured out of the van and blinked in the harsh sunlight. Three weeks of underground training in florescent lighting made the sun seem unnaturally bright.

The van crawled away and clacked over the planks of the bridge, then sped off. We squinted at each other, the Keepers. Kate rescued a lady bug off of Mel's shoulder and shook it into the wind. Mel wrapped her arm around Kate's waist and they put their heads together, brunette and blond, in a private conversation ending in giggles. I turned to Mel's husband, the tall lanky Donnie Dudgeon, and we shook our heads. Kate and Mel seemed destined to giggle when they got together. Trip shifted reaching for the sword normally strapped to his side, his fist closed on air. He let out a frustrated huff and gazed over the hills, ever vigilant. Tara, a goddess-like creature, squared off at his shoulder, scanning the opposite direction. Dirk swung his backpack onto his back, then cracked his knuckles.

Our mission firm in our minds, we were the task force trained to save the village from the mysterious saboteur; four teens and three barely out of their teens, with thousands of years of life experience shared between us. We would enter quantum jumps to ascertain which of the 12 Inner Circle members had gone rogue and started sabotaging the jump therapy sessions.

"I guess that's our ride into the village." Dirk pointed, his muscled arm flexing beneath coffee colored skin, to a large hay-stuffed wagon hitched to a pair of charcoal-tinted mules.

Kate stretched and shifted her backpack, cutting her eyes to me in a playful grin. "I am so glad to be outside again." She spun in a circle and fell into my arms.

Donnie howled and tossed Mel over his shoulder. She squealed like a child while he pranced around the parking lot. We hooted at them and moved toward the trailer.

"Hey, Gladiator G.I. Joe!" Kate released my hand and skipped forward, calling to Trip.

He stopped and turned a baleful glare onto her. "I told you not to call me that, Katie girl." He cracked a smile when she jumped onto his back.

"I just want a piggyback ride to round out the whole farm-slash-hay-ride experience." She roughed up his hair and he locked his arms under her legs and trotted off.

"So if he is Gladiator G.I. Joe," I rubbed my palm over my chin and sized up Tara, the statuesque dragon slayer. "Then that makes you Xena Warrior Barbie."

"Corey Chastain, you did not just call me that!" She arched her brow and swatted at me. I ran backwards to the hay-filled wagon, taunting her.

Grinning as Tara caught up to me with a punch, I caught Kate when she tumbled off of Trip's back and into my arms. We burrowed down under the straw sniggering and stealing kisses until the others caught up and climbed aboard. Dirk, our fearless leader, pretended to step on us to get to the driver's seat. Then launching up from the hay, we attacked him, burying him in mounds of the stuff. An all-out alfalfa war ensued, strewing hay all over the road.

Dirk escaped, took up the reins, and whistled to the mules. The wagon rocked forward and Kate fell into my arms, giggling. We dove under the golden blanket again. Ah, the taste of Kate's lips—

"Get a room!" Trip growled, arm hanging over Tara's shoulder. Kate flushed and kissed me again before crawling out to bask in the sunshine as the wagon jostled us toward the village. Kate tilted her face to the sun. I picked straw out of her hair and gazed over the campus.

The day beamed a bright sky as vibrant as a field of bluebonnets. Tara's golden hair reflected in the sunlight as she shifted on the hay bale to lean back against Trip's chest. Trip's usual scowl paused when he pressed his chin to the top of her head, then resumed as he plucked a straw and set it between his teeth. Mel and Donnie sat at the end of the wagon with their legs dangling off. Mel leaned back on her elbows and let the sun warm her cheeks. She hummed a familiar tune, pale hair the color of Tara's and mine wafted in the breeze. We watched the beauty of the summer drift by to the accompaniment of croakers and chirpers.

It felt so good to be out of that underground bunker. Three weeks of constant training, memorizing files, and testing as jump commanders without a peek of sunlight drove us stir crazy. A bit giddy, we soaked in the honeysuckle air and acted our physical ages for a change.

We spent our hibernation in intense physical and mental training, side by side, giving Kate a chance to get close to everyone on the team. That included Trip. They were already pretty tight, but we felt if our mission to expose the infiltrator was going to succeed, then Kate needed freedom to spend time with all of us equally. Counting on her uncanny intuition on the jumps, we all opened ourselves to her. Her innate ability to love unconditionally without reservation bonded us to her, the secret keeper. Her ability to care for others amazed me, and seeing the whole team attached to her gave me joy. Mostly.

I shrugged dark thoughts away. I just wanted to enjoy this awesome day with my girl. I pecked Kate on the cheek and slung my arm over her shoulders. She slowly blinked at me and pressed her palm against mine. We laced our fingers together. She held my gaze, her pupils wide with emotion. She drew closer, trapping me in her intensity. Nothing satisfied me like her love-filled expression. Nothing captured me like her pure attention focused solely on me. She drew a shaky breath and turned her face back to the sun and nestled her head against my shoulder.

The screeching sphere descended suddenly. Vacuumed into swirling light fractals swishing around us like whitewater rapids, we were abducted and then dumped at the edge of a cliff. A sheer drop to a rock-strewn beach below reminded me of Kate's jump when she had faced the Daddy monster three weeks earlier. This was not the same world, though. Only one sun lit the sky here.

People dressed in drab garb wandered the plain around us. Listless and dull they roamed without purpose.

"Okay, Keepers, eyes peeled." Dirk turned a slow circle, making sure we were all accounted for.

Kate pressed against my side and I took her hand. She tucked her hair behind her ear. "Why have we jumped? We aren't supposed to be activated, yet, right?" She reached her other hand to touch Mel's arm reassuringly.

"Mama Ty said we were going to go to the Scriptorium first," Mel murmured as she scanned the people milling around.

The Scriptorium existed on two planes, the cave under the gazebo in the heart-shaped lake and a portal to an immortal world. Jump teams went to receive instruction, a spiritual preparation for their time at Heartwork Village. Since we had been separated from the Chartreuse team to form a secret task force called The Keepers, we still needed to go there. We didn't even know who would be in charge.

"I told you we should have kept our weapons!" Trip spat and shifted his stance, back to back with Tara, both in full warrior mode.

"Guys, check it out." Donnie pointed over the edge of the cliff to the ocean and we all turned our attention to the foaming waves as they rolled in to crash against the rocks.

An enormous head rose out of the billowing sea, horns first. Salt spray crashed around it and streamed down the massive scales as feral orbs blinked open. It rose quickly revealing the colossal giant of a monster as it lurched toward us. Muscled arms the size of dual stadiums jutted from his slimy torso. A tail crashed behind him causing tsunami like waves to fracture and speed in opposite directions.

He halted with one foot in the ocean and the other foot on the land, threw back his head and bellowed. Darkness spewed from his mouth to blot out the sky. The people screamed and ran in all directions, panic-stricken and chaotic. Some ran off the cliff edge and fell to crunch on the rocks far below.

The monster took a swipe at the cliff and the earth crumbled into the ocean taking dozens of people down with it and catapulting others into us. Kate and Mel, hit by a flying man, sailed down the hill. I turned to run after them when the ground beneath my feet gave way.

Darkened sky descended in black fog pillars to eclipse the day, and I couldn't discern the black loam of the cliff from the inky darkness. I scrambled, clawing and grabbing to keep from spilling over the ragged edge.

We were thrown into midnight with screams and wails as our only orientation. Descending shrieks and crashing waves far below chased me toward chaotic moans and shouts above.

"Corey!" I heard Trip's voice above the chaos. It sounded near.

"Here!" I clung to the side of the precipice.

"Take my hand!"

"I can't see you, Trip!"

"I'm here. I'm right here."

He sounded so close. I trusted Trip with my life, he'd become one of my best friends over the last three weeks. I wouldn't be able to hang on much longer. I drew a deep breath, released the root I dangled from, and arced my hand into the darkness above me.

I hit solid muscle and felt it clamp around my forearm.

He lifted me slowly and I pumped my legs into the side of the cliff. Together we made purchase until I collapsed on the ground beside him. He clutched my shoulder in one of his large palms and gripped my forearm.

"Thanks," I huffed. "Thanks."

He pounded my shoulder and lifted me up.

"Kate. Where is Kate?" I breathed heavily as we rose to stand side by side in the darkness.

The roar of the monster muffled Trip's reply. So dark, I checked my step, afraid to move. We could step right off the edge if we tried to move in the absolute darkness.

A flicker drew my attention. I looked down at my chest. A reddish golden glow emanated from the center of my frame. I followed the light trail to see Trip's face illuminated by the radiance. His mouth hung open and his eyes grew round as he stared at the light coming from me.

Other faces appeared in the circle around us. Kate, Tara, Mel, Donnie, Dirk and the strangers were drawn to the only circumference of light left in this world. Trip reached out and touched my shirt where the light centered and it skimmed up his arm and landed in the middle of his chest, flashing a brilliant white, then simmering to the golden glow.

Our eyes met.

"Whoa," he whispered and turned his hand around to gawk at the luminosity staining his fingertips.

A loud screech enveloped us, and then deposited us on the black-top road beside the hay wagon. We staggered, trying to gain our bearings.

"Wha what just happened?" Kate squinted her eyes against the sudden brightness. A trickle of blood flowed from a gash on her temple. I moved toward her just as she gasped and turned toward Mel. "Mel, are you okay?"

Mel swayed on her feet. Donnie and Kate, nearest her, rushed to take her by the elbows and assist her to the flatbed trailer.

I grabbed the first aid kit from the storage under the driver's seat and ran to the back of the wagon. I dabbed at Kate's face with gauze while she fussed and crooned over her friend. "Mel sit here. Drink this water." She cracked the seal of a bottle of water and pressed it to Mel's lips.

"I'm fine." Mel waved us away. "Just got dizzy." But she accepted the water bottle from Kate and sipped again.

Kate took the cloth from me with a sweet smile and pressed it against her wound. "Thank you, Corey." She kissed my cheek and left a burning imprint where her lips touched. Then she turned back to Mel, Donnie and Tara to make sure they were okay.

I urged Dirk and Trip to the side. "What just happen?"

Dirk slowly wagged his head back and forth. "Unprecedented. Never happened before."

"What do you mean? We get ripped out of this place all the friggin' time." Trip's arms were covered in the same black soil as me.

"No, not just the jump, though we aren't on active status. Quantum Spheres shouldn't be forming yet. The weird part is being dumped in the middle of the campus. We're supposed to reappear in the QHR."

The quantum jumps always took us back to the Quantum Home Room for detox. "Obviously this wasn't a sanctioned jump," I said.

"So the infiltrator sent us there?" Trip asked.

Dirk shrugged. "Let's get to the QHR."

I rubbed at my chest. A tingling sensation remained where the light had blazed.

# ABOUT THE AUTHOR

LaDonna Cole thrives in the Smoky Mountains of Tennessee with her children, singing, writing and traveling as much as possible. A Psychiatric Nurse and incurable optimist, she draws on her zest for adventure, passion for family, and journey through faith to release the soul of each new story.

COMING
TO AUDIO

# THE
# TORN

THE
## TORN

BOOK ONE OF THE HOLDING KATE SERIES

LaDonna Cole
NARRATED BY AMANDA MARIER

NARRATED BY
AMANDA MARIER

www.ingramcontent.com/pod-product-compliance
Lightning Source LLC
Chambersburg PA
CBHW020628130626
46552CB00003B/1124